P9-CDI-857

She didn't want to die.

She punched the number on speed dial.

Ian answered.

The urge to cry slammed into Maggie. "Ian, it's me."

"Maggie?" Surprise flooded his voice. "Are you okay?"

"He was going to kill me, Ian. He's already killed four women."

"You saw him?" Ian asked, shocked. "He was that close?"

"I watched him working his way to the door." She forced her voice. "Tonight was going to be the night."

Ian sucked in a sharp breath. "Are you safe now?"

"He's eager to get me out of the way. It's time."

"Time for what?"

"For him to kill again." Her breath stuttered. "Before the end of December, he'll kill again." All four murders had been in December, a week either side of Christmas.

"All the more reason to come home and let me help."

Ian's voice. She hated to admit just how badly she needed to hear it.

Books by Vicki Hinze

Love Inspired Suspense

*Survive the Night
*Christmas Countdown

*Lost, Inc.

VICKI HINZE

is an award-winning author of nearly thirty novels, four nonfiction books and hundreds of articles published in as many as sixty-three countries. She lives in Florida with her husband, near her children and grands, and she gets cranky if she must miss one of their ball games. Vicki loves to visit with readers and invites you to join her at vickihinze.com or on Facebook.

Christmas
COUNTDOWN

VICKI HINZE

Love Inspired

If you purchased this book without a cover you should be aware that this book is stolen property. It was reported as "unsold and destroyed" to the publisher, and neither the author nor the publisher has received any payment for this "stripped book."

Recycling programs for this product may not exist in your area.

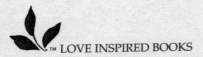

™ LOVE INSPIRED BOOKS

ISBN-13: 978-0-373-44517-2

CHRISTMAS COUNTDOWN

Copyright © 2012 by Vicki Hinze

All rights reserved. Except for use in any review, the reproduction or utilization of this work in whole or in part in any form by any electronic, mechanical or other means, now known or hereafter invented, including xerography, photocopying and recording, or in any information storage or retrieval system, is forbidden without the written permission of the editorial office, Love Inspired Books, 233 Broadway, New York, NY 10279 U.S.A.

This is a work of fiction. Names, characters, places and incidents are either the product of the author's imagination or are used fictitiously, and any resemblance to actual persons, living or dead, business establishments, events or locales is entirely coincidental.

This edition published by arrangement with Love Inspired Books.

® and TM are trademarks of Love Inspired Books, used under license. Trademarks indicated with ® are registered in the United States Patent and Trademark Office, the Canadian Trade Marks Office and in other countries.

www.LoveInspiredBooks.com

Printed in U.S.A.

Greater love hath no man than this,
that a man lay down his life for his friends.
—*John* 15:13

To Dawn Woodhams,
an admirable heroine very much like Maggie.
With love and wishes for much joy and many...
Blessings,
Vicki

ONE

Something wasn't right.

Alert and armed, Maggie Mason moved room to room. Outwardly nothing appeared to be wrong. The house was chilly and quiet, silent in the way a house is on a cold December night when you're in it alone. Yet the awareness that something was off prodded her honed instincts. You didn't work in her field, much less enjoy her success, and not hone your instincts or fail to respect them. No one was inside the house with her; she'd have picked up on that immediately. Yet some nebulous alert had triggered her internal alarm. She couldn't explain it. She just felt it.

Knew it.

Feared it.

And she'd learned the hard way to never ignore internal warnings.

Controlling her breathing, deliberately working to slow her racing heart, she circled back to the kitchen, clicked on her flashlight and followed her emergency plan, taking the worn wooden stairs down to the basement. An unadvertised and unmentioned feature in the basement sold her on renting the Decatur, Illinois, home just days ago. It wasn't in the best neighborhood, but she'd lived in far worse, and it had that nondescript look about it—not too nice, not too dumpy—where she could fade into obscurity.

Obscurity was essential.

With it and any luck, she wouldn't have to move again for a couple of months. Oh, how she yearned for a little luck.

In the past three years, her record for staying put, hospital and recovery time aside, was two months, fourteen days, seven hours and twelve minutes. This basement's special feature could help buy her a little more time here and help her break her record. At least, she dared to hope it could.

Please, God. I'm so tired of running.

A knot rose in her throat. She swallowed it down and stepped off the bottom stair onto the cracked concrete floor. The twenty-by-twenty open area billed as a basement storage room was inky dark—no electricity, no windows, and only one door at the top of the stairs she'd just descended...or so it appeared until further inspection.

Sweeping the beam of light corner to corner on the floor, she checked the dull coating of dust for new footprints but spotted none, then lifted the beam up the walls, casting light on the thin cobwebs clinging to the corners at the ceiling and on the floor joists overhead. The webs glistened but remained intact.

A little reassured, she eased her finger on the trigger of her weapon and took a steadying breath to work the hitch from her chest. The basement clearly had been abandoned for a long time, yet it didn't smell musty or dank. Odd, with the occasional water stain in the pink fiberglass insulation stuffed between the wall studs. The stains spoke of past leaks now repaired, but the absence of a musty scent had first alerted her that more than met the eye was in this basement.

Following the flashlight beam, she moved across the empty expanse to the back wall, where a tall and rickety wooden shelving unit stood in the corner. Battered and worn, it, too, wore a layer of dust she'd been careful not to disturb. She checked each shelf. No smears or swipes marring its dull surface. Here, too, the dust remained undisturbed.

Stretching on tiptoes, she reached between the top and second shelves and tapped seeking fingertips along the rough wooden back wall. They snagged metal. A flathead bolt. Inching her nails under its edge, she pulled the bolt out and then slid the entire shelving unit sideways. Gliders bore its weight, but it moved in jerked spurts.

In the wall where the unit had stood, an opening appeared: a low, narrow passageway.

At one time, that passageway likely had been used as an emergency exit for a drug dealer—she'd seen a number of those in neighborhoods such as this during her time as a normal, active FBI profiler—but the rental agent hadn't mentioned the passageway at all. When he'd left her to explore, she'd found it on her own, though she hadn't mentioned finding it to him, either. If he'd known, he'd have disclosed it. For her own safety, the fewer who knew the better.

Bending low to keep from cracking her head against the wooden-beam reinforcements holding back the earth inside the tunnel, she focused her flashlight's beam down the passage and then followed it to its abrupt end at a heavy metal grate. The first thing she'd done when she moved in was to replace the grate lock with one of her own. She peered through the lacy metal outside into the backs of thick, squat bushes. The grate couldn't be seen from the yard. It took knowing it was there behind the bushes to find it.

She carefully checked the grate's internal perimeter. The chewing gum embedded with a single strand of hair she'd pressed on each of the four corners remained untouched and in place. Peering outside again, she scanned the dirt behind the bushes and spotted the heavy-duty string she'd strung ankle-high. Unmoved. Nothing disrupted the smooth dirt, and the stones she'd arranged in a distinct pattern were exactly where she'd put them.

Her escape route was intact.

Yet her internal alarm didn't shut off. It continued to pound its warning in time with the fast beats of her heart.

You've been running too long, Maggie.

She had. And paranoia was setting in. Chiding herself, she made her way back upstairs then bolted the basement door, slamming home both original dead bolts and the one she'd installed the night she'd moved in. *Three days and counting...*

Breathing easier, she tucked her weapon into the holster at the back of her jeans' waistband and shifted her focus to the barren kitchen. A familiar ache settled in her chest. It lacked any of the warmth or comfort of generations of family use. The kitchen on the ranch in North Bay, Florida, on the other hand, held a lot of history. Most of her history. It was and always had been home. Her big brother, Paul, still lived there, but for now, home and North Bay were off-limits to her. If Gary Crawford had anything to say about it, both would remain off-limits to her for the rest of her life, which he had every intention of ending as soon as possible.

Resentment and bitterness welled up from deep in-side and soured her stomach.

No, don't do it, Maggie. Don't. Think about some-thing else.

She looked at the kitchen table. Its once-white enamel top was chipped and yellowed and worn slick but the table was still sturdy, and currently nearly buried under the strewn makings of a gingerbread house. Christmas was just weeks away—the fourth in a row she'd spend alone—but she'd kept the gingerbread house family tra-dition for the past three, and she would keep it for this one, too. It wasn't much, but when you had nothing, it was, well, *something*.

Running was never easy. But holidays were hardest.

Her eyes burned. She blinked fast and snipped the corner of a Ziploc bag, inserted the plastic piping tip and seated it, then spooned icing into the bag. At home, Paul had always stuffed the icing bag. She'd put the gumdrops on the house, sprinkle nuts around the base and position the candy canes to frame the front door.

A smile curved her lips. From the time she'd had to tiptoe to reach the tabletop, Paul had fawned over her perfectly positioning each gumdrop. Every girl should be so lucky as to have a brother like him. She sniffed and checked her watch—4:10. He was late calling her, but just ten minutes. Not yet worrisomely late.

Snagging an apple, she took a crunchy bite, discov-ered she was starved and scarfed it down, then tossed the core into the trash can under the sink and rinsed her hands, careful not to bump the cup filled with her best artist's paintbrushes beside the tap. She gave them a longing look. *Security first. Then the gingerbread house. Then landscapes.* "Just a little longer," she told the red cup of brushes. "Tomorrow night, I paint. Maybe that sunset in Lafitte, Louisiana." The fall of dusk and the fading light on the bayou had been stunning...

Finally at 5:15 her cell phone rang.

Brushing at an errant lock of long reddish-blond hair clinging to her cheek, she primed to give Paul a hard time for calling late and checked caller ID. It was Ian. At first, he was her brother's good friend from the military, a physician and husband to Maggie's now-deceased friend, Beth. Now Ian was an investigator at Lost, Inc. And while due to Beth's murder he'd pushed most people away, he and Maggie remained close. But why was he calling now? Was something wrong with Paul?

Don't jump to conclusions. You've got enough trouble without borrowing more. "Ian, how are you?"

"Hi, Maggie. Paul's out of pocket and I promised him I'd check in on you. Sorry I'm late. Got tied up with a client. You okay?"

"For the moment." Trying not to be disappointed Ian called her as a favor, she pulled out a chair at the table. It scudded across the wooden floor. "Where's Paul?" Her brother rarely missed an appointed call with her. "He's okay, isn't—"

"He's fine. He and Della are on their way to her stepgrandmother's." Ian sounded excited.

"Did he propose to her or something?" Maggie snitched a red gumdrop. Paul hadn't told her, so she doubted it, but with the move, she had been out of touch the better part of two weeks.

"I think that might be the reason for the trip. She's Della's closest relative."

Paul would ask *somebody's* permission first, so it fit. He'd loved Della Jackson for two years, but she'd only recently allowed herself to love anyone. Thank goodness, she'd chosen Paul. He deserved the best, and Maggie prayed every day he got it. "I hope it is."

"Either way, they're happy and celebrating."

"If he hasn't proposed yet, what are they celebrating?"

"The hunt is over, Maggie." Intense emotion thickened Ian's deep voice.

Over. She tensed, afraid to hope. "They've caught Gary Crawford?" Surely she'd have heard through FBI channels—

"No. No, I'm sorry." Ian let out a powerful sigh, clearly rebuking himself for raising and then dashing her hopes. "They caught Della's stalker."

Disappointment fell to confusion. "It wasn't Crawford?" Maggie crunched a crisp piece of gingerbread between her forefinger and thumb. The entire task force agreed the stalker had to be Crawford. "You're sure?"

"Positive. It was Jeff Jackson, Della's ex. They had a personal encounter, and police nailed him with hard evidence."

"Personal encounter?" Sounded dangerous. She knew just how dangerous close encounters with Crawford could be, and how good he was at setting up others to take blame for his actions. Had he done that in this case? He'd nearly killed her with a car bomb in Utah. The shrapnel did what was expected to be permanent injury to her leg. Months in the hospital, multiple surgeries and more months of physical therapy, where she'd worked to the point of exhaustion to recover—her survival required mobility. She had ninety percent success in function of her leg as opposed to the forty-five percent the doctors originally estimated. Now there was another *personal encounter?* Elated and deflated simultaneously, Maggie pressed her elbow on the table and braced her head in her hand. "Paul and Della weren't hurt—"

"No, they're fine. They're great. I told you they're celebrating."

Life. They were living a life without being hunted down like animals. Living and laughing and loving... Maggie's eyes burned again, and again she blinked hard. She wanted those things for Paul, of course. Problem was, she wanted them for herself, too.

Pipe dream.

Definitely a pipe dream, and it would be so long as Gary Crawford drew breath.

She turned her mind and focused on letting gladness fill her heart. "I'm happy for them." So it was Jeff Jackson, not Gary Crawford. "They have to be breathing a lot easier."

"Paul won't breathe easy until you come home."

Guilt speared her. She stared sightlessly at the white stove top. Home. Safety. Security. The beloved ranch she'd grown up on, the rescue animals Paul had taken in for her, the friends she'd known her whole life, the smell of the pines and the feel of the grass and sandy beach under her feet at the little creek. Longing burned her stomach and left it hollow. More than anything she wanted to go home. Well, more than anything except not to ever again endanger those she loved. Her throat thick, she swallowed. "I wish I could, but I can't, Ian. You know why."

A year ago in Utah, Crawford had nearly killed both Paul and her in an act of revenge against her. He was a serial killer. A very bright one who had murdered four women and she'd been called in to profile him. She'd picked up things others had missed, giving the task force needed insights that brought them too close to cap-

turing him, and he resented it enough to want her dead.
Crawford willingly used those she loved as bait to get
to her. If Paul hadn't forgotten his phone and gone back
to get it and she hadn't started her car using the remote,
he would have succeeded. It'd taken her six months to
recuperate and get out from under intense medical care.
No way was she exposing Paul to that again. Her heart
couldn't take the trauma or bear the guilt.

"How's your leg?" Ian asked. "Doing the exercises
like you're supposed to?"

She smiled. "Yes, and with the move, a lot more."
Since his wife's—her friend's—murder three years ago,
he and Maggie had supported each other long-distance.
Little happened in either's life that the other wasn't
aware of—her job status aside. That she couldn't share.
"How's Uncle Warny?"

"He wants you to come home, too."

"You're as bad as Paul with the guilt trips, Ian Crane.
You know Crawford is still after me. I can't come home,
so quit."

"I know why you *think* you can't come home. You're
protecting everybody else. But, Maggie, think about it.
Paul and I and everyone at Lost, Inc., are ex-military
and investigative specialists. We can protect ourselves,
and we can help protect you."

Her childhood friend Madison McKay, a POW sacrificed to avert an international incident, had escaped
and returned home to start the agency for the sole purpose of helping others who were lost find their way
home. "You can't. Crawford proved that in Utah. But I
know you, and I know Paul. This is about you two wanting to protect me." Paul had always protected her and,
since Beth's passing while Ian was still active duty in

the military and deployed to Afghanistan, he wanted to protect *everybody*.

"You can't run forever, Maggie."

She squeezed her eyes shut. "Not running doesn't work. If I come home, it means everyone I care about spends every moment looking back over his or her shoulder, and I worry nonstop when and where and whom Crawford is going to strike next. All of you deserve better. This is my problem. I'll deal with it."

"Will you just let me say what I have to say? I know you're tired of hearing it, but I'm not going to make the same old argument—I promise."

Ian was a former flight surgeon. After Beth's death, he left both medicine and the military and went to work at Lost, Inc., as an investigator. Paul, a former special operations officer, now worked as a veterans' advocate. Both men had special skills and abilities and could help her, and they wanted to, yet didn't they realize that's exactly why she couldn't endanger them? If she lost them, she lost everything. She could talk freely with Ian in ways she couldn't talk with Paul, who'd been more parent than brother to her for her whole life. She couldn't lose either of them, and Crawford would use that. Still, Ian needed to have his say. "Go ahead."

"You really can't run forever. Crawford only has to be right once. You have to be right every single time. One mistake…" A hard edge nicked his voice. "We've seen what one mistake can do." He paused, no doubt to give her time to remember—not that she needed it. Who could forget?

"Think about something else, too," Ian went on. "Della didn't run and it worked out. She's not a prisoner anymore. She's free, Maggie. I want you to be free, too."

A hard lump crept higher, swelling in her throat.

She grabbed a soda from the fridge and shut the door with her hip. "I'm seriously happy it worked out for her, but Jeff Jackson isn't a mastermind serial killer. Gary Crawford is." Maggie popped the top on the can. A swooshed gush of compressed air rushed out. "He's killed four women—that we know of—and he's determined to kill me."

"Which is exactly why you should come home. Maggie, listen to me. Please. Let us help you. We *can* help." He rushed his words as if afraid he wouldn't get them spoken before she tuned him out. "Paul and Della teamed up with the staff at Lost, Inc., and we won. If we did it for Della, we can do it for you. We're trained for this. We *can* do it."

Her heart ached. For three years, Ian had been struggling to care about something. The grief of losing Beth had tried its best to rob the joy of life from him. Maggie had refused to let it. Now he had that same desolate tone about her and her situation. Not good, that. Yet he had a point. Madison McKay, the owner of Lost, Inc., had been Maggie's friend since birth. They'd grown up together. The others at Lost, Inc., were newcomers Maggie didn't know well, but for Paul, they would put their lives on the line and protect her. Maybe together, all of them could battle Crawford and win.

Temptation bit her hard. She resisted it, and it bit her again. Harder. She could go home. Be with her family, her friends, Ian. No more holidays alone. No more running, always being on guard, always looking back, worrying about every move, every action. *Peace. Calm. Safety.* It would be so easy to say yes. So easy…

And so wrong.

No. No, she couldn't do it. Not and watch Gary Crawford murder them for sport, to terrify her, and just to show her he could. The entire FBI hadn't been able to protect her, which had driven her undercover, relying on them only for ancillary support. No. So long as she could stay a step ahead of him, she had to keep trying to face him alone. He wasn't killing other women while tied up chasing her. She couldn't forget that. If a time came when she couldn't do it and putting them in jeopardy by asking for their help was an essential last resort to her survival, then she'd seek their help. Yet Crawford now seemed to know whatever the FBI did, and considering that, her survival odds would be better with her friends and family to protect her. But she could risk their help only as an essential last resort.

Who are you kidding? Could you jeopardize them even then, Maggie? Well, could you?

Her hand shook. She wasn't sure. But Ian needed that reassurance. He needed her promise.

"Did you hear me, Maggie?"

"I heard you." She shoved at the gumdrops, pushing them in place on the gingerbread house.

He sighed. "The reward for being great at your job shouldn't be a penalty that robs you of a life."

"My former job." After the Utah bombing, she'd publicly retired from the FBI and gone undercover. Officially and on paper, she wasn't profiling anymore, just painting landscapes. They'd hoped that would get Crawford off her back. It hadn't made any difference to him. She'd homed in on things in his first four murders that others had missed. Things that brought her and the FBI task force close to his door, and he resented it enough to vow he wouldn't rest until he'd killed her. He had made serious efforts to make good on his word. And she'd vowed to find him first and had made serious efforts to make good on *her* word. The net effect was that sometimes she was the cat and sometimes she was the mouse. If she could just peg the significance of his black rose, she'd win this test of wills and skills between them. She knew she would. It had to be key.

He'd given a black rose to only one living victim—his second. And twice, he'd left a black rose for Maggie. Both times, she'd known he was close and had retreated to regroup. But even now she didn't understand the stealth message in that flower. Why would a man bent on killing you telegraph that he'd located you? Why did he kill and then deliver a dozen Black Beauty roses to his victim after burial? She just didn't get it, and until she did, she was stuck in the cat-and-mouse maze, matching wits with a skilled serial killer so accomplished he terrified seasoned pros.

"Your former job." Ian sighed. "It's nearly Christmas, Maggie. I don't want to spend another one knowing you're alone and Paul and your uncle Warny are looking across the table at your empty chair. And you and me talking while we eat just isn't the same. You know Warny would love you being home for Christmas."

Warny. She imagined her elderly uncle, wearing his overalls, his flannel shirts, his baseball cap and the ever-present red-and-white bandanna half hanging out of his back pocket. Her resolve drained, weakening. She wanted to go home. She wanted to sit in her chair and live her life with her family. She wanted to not run, not live with a knot of fear in her stomach all the time. To never again get another phone call from that twisted killer where all he did was taunt her, flaunting it that he was the cat and she the mouse. Chills ran up and down her arms, her back. She wanted to be normal again, and Ian offered it to her. The problem was, in accepting it she could be signing his death warrant. That shored up her thready resolve and gave her the strength and courage to turn her back on what she wanted and opt for what was right.

Tears flowed down her cheeks and regret dampened her tone. "I'd love nothing more, but you know...I can't." She gulped in air. "I'll call soon."

Before Ian could tempt her more, she hung up the phone. Sitting alone at the table, she stared at the lopsided gingerbread house and wept until dark.

He'd pushed her too hard.

Maggie had ended their call abruptly and too soon. His fault. Why had he pushed so hard? *Why?*

Ian sat in his lamp-lit living room and reread Maggie's note. She'd saved it as a draft in their joint email account—they never sent anything to avoid being traced—nearly a week ago, and he'd rather have talked to her a while longer, but the note would have to do.

On the move again. Will let you know when I've landed. Ian, it means so much to me to be able to write you. I have to watch what I say to Paul because, well, he's my big brother, and if he knew how close Crawford has come to getting me lately, he'd lose his mind.

Did you get the photo I uploaded? What do you think of the new look? Hair's still long, but red. Well, reddish. Isn't it wild?

Thanksgiving was awful and the Christmas countdown has begun. Holidays are the loneliest days now. Watching others with their families...I can hardly stand it. I'm happy for them, but sad for me. I hate being isolated but, as you so often say, things are what they are. At least once every season, I indulge in a blowout pity party. An unfettered squalling session where I shovel in an entire quart of Ben & Jerry's Chocolate Fudge Brownie ice cream during a two-hour bath immersed in bubbles using hot water with zero regard for neighbors sharing the water heater. It's just total self-indulgence and me. (I'll rent a house this time to not inconvenience anyone else. With luck, I'll get to stay in it until after Christmas.)

Binging doesn't help and afterward, I feel guilty for being a hot-water hog, sick from eating too many sweets, and my head hurts for a full day from crying. It's ridiculous, and every time I ask why I do that to myself, but next holiday season, I do it again. Too, I confess that even a self-indulgent blowout pity party without someone there to hold you and tell you not to worry, that things will be all right, makes you feel even more alone. This Christmas I'm going to try to skip it. I've been praying on it for weeks already, but I don't know if my heart is in the right place. My main reason is that I don't need the added stress. Do you think God will be sympathetic to that and help me? I can't do it on my own, so I hope He is and does.

What will you be doing? I need to hear something normal. You know how fish-out-of-water I feel when I move. I need grounding, and I'm counting on you. Don't you feel lucky?
Love,
Maggie

A lump rose in Ian's throat. She'd now moved and he still hadn't responded to the note. He couldn't. He didn't have the heart to answer her email draft with a reply draft telling her he felt every bit as lonely and isolated as she did. Or that he'd be spending the holiday at home alone, indulging in his own pity party sans the ice cream and bubble bath. He'd be teetering on the edge of the depression abyss and rereading her cards and email drafts to pull him back to solid ground.

She'd fuss at him for wasting his life in self-imposed isolation when she craved company. Worse, she'd cry. He didn't have to see her to know it. Maggie Mason was a strong but tenderhearted woman, and him doing what he did on holidays would strum her fragile strings. She rarely cried, but she would over that and the idea that he'd put Maggie in tears after all she'd been through and was still going through...he couldn't stand it.

Yet after that botched phone call, he had to answer her with *something*. Tell her *something* to lift her spirits. Moving to a new place was hard on her, and she'd had a rash of moves in the past year. Crawford was figuring out how her mind worked, and that made an already dangerous situation even more so for her. She needed to come home, where he and Paul could help her. Ian swept an unsteady hand across his forehead. It was worse than that. When Maggie admitted she was struggling, she was *really* struggling. He'd never known such a steely, courageous woman. Beth had been no slouch, but during his deployment to Afghanistan, she'd leaned hard on Maggie, and Maggie had been there for her, just as she had been there for him since Beth's death.

And her devotion to others was repaid with Gary Crawford stealing her life.

Anger simmered in Ian. Maggie deserved better. So much better...and so much more. If Ian still prayed, he'd pray for Maggie. For something to happen so Crawford couldn't hunt or hurt her ever again. He swiped a damp hand along his jean-clad thigh. But he didn't pray anymore. He hadn't since Beth's murder. And unless her murderer was found, convicted and justice prevailed, he doubted he'd ever pray again.

He'd done his part, going to Afghanistan and doctoring the sick and wounded. Not once had he asked God to spare his life. Not once. All he'd asked was that God protect his wife. But He hadn't. Ian had been in a war zone, but Beth had been murdered in her own home. The police figured it was some drug addict who knew Ian was a doctor, looking for painkillers.

He'd loved, honored and cherished, but he'd failed to protect her.

Guilt clawed his insides raw. Staring at his reflection in the glossy wooden tabletop beside his easy chair, he gave in to regret, suffered the hopelessness and helplessness for a long minute. Then, teetering at the edge of the abyss, he sought solace by lifting the worn page and reading Maggie's note yet again.

Love, Maggie. His heart hitched. She did deserve better and more, and though he felt totally incapable of giving her either, she was counting on him. She'd chosen him as her confidant. His best was pathetic, paltry. Man, he wished she had made a wiser choice. But she hadn't. She'd chosen him, no doubt due to her relationship with Beth, and he owed her. He'd give her all he had. "Okay, Doc," he told himself. "Rise to the occasion. Put your heart into it."

Fear rippled up his back, tingled in the roof of his mouth. He'd failed Beth and barely survived it. He couldn't fail Maggie, too. Yet putting his heart into anything was a tall order. The urge to shrink away hit him hard. His every instinct said backing away was right, smart and necessary to him making it through another day. Opening your heart led to unspeakable pain, and he'd already had his share and more. Still, he couldn't shrink away or turn his back. He couldn't. This was Maggie.

She always remembered him—his birthday, Christmas, the anniversary of Beth's death. Maggie talked him through the hardest times of his life and never missed a chance to congratulate or encourage him. The wear on her often-read cards and printed email drafts proved how sorely he needed what she freely gave him and how heavily he relied on her. Wasn't *she* the lucky one?

He took a sip of the cool coffee in his cup then set it back onto the stone coaster. Maggie needed him. She'd faithfully been there for Beth and him. Now he had to be there for her.

"Think, Ian. Think." Still blanking out on what to say, he pushed himself hard then harder. More than three years had passed since Beth died, and losing her remained an open wound that kept him nearly emotionally paralyzed. Anyone else in a similar circumstance to Maggie he'd refer to Madison McKay or Paul, but this time that wasn't an option. Maggie couldn't be totally open with Madison, a lifelong friend, or her brother.

You're too messed up. You'd die for her, yeah. But give her anything with emotion, and actually live? No way. You're DOA, Doc.

Fear twisted like a knife inside him. His hand shook. He could be DOA, but he had to try. Desperate, he whispered, "God, don't You dare let her down. She still believes in You."

God likely would take care of Maggie. He had kept her alive so far. But would He? And could Ian give her what she needed? Truth was truth, and he couldn't survive that kind of failure, or the guilt that came with it, twice.

Mess up, and you're down for the count.

"Don't tempt me," he told himself. Death was easy. Living was tough.

The doorbell rang.

Ian set aside Maggie's note and hauled himself out of his chair. General Talbot and Colonel Dayton had arrived to watch the ball game. It was a tradition they'd begun when Ian worked at the base on active duty, before he'd gone to Afghanistan. After Beth's death and his return home, he'd tried to nix the get-togethers but the commanders, under the guise of being supportive, refused to let him, so he tolerated it.

There had been a security breach at the Nest, the top-secret military facility hidden deep within the wooded confines of the base under Talbot and Dayton's command. Considering that they were looking at Ian and everyone else at Lost, Inc., the investigative firm he'd worked at since leaving active duty, for someone to blame for that breach to protect their careers and pending promotions, now wasn't a good time to alienate the commanders.

Resigned, Ian opened the door.

One week later...

The doorbell rang.

Maggie's heart slammed against her ribs. She sat straight up in bed, snagged her weapon from under her pillow and crammed her flashlight into the pocket of her jeans. She hadn't gone to bed in PJs in three years, but always slept fully dressed, prepared for nights with an incident like this.

Hyperalert, she listened for the bell to chime again. It didn't. She hadn't dreamed it. She never slept soundly at night; if anything, she just dozed. Crawford attacked at night. The ring was real—and unexpected. The only person in Decatur who knew her at all was the rental agent, and there was no reason he'd be ringing her bell at midnight.

Midnight. Exactly, according to the red numerals on her bedside clock. *The precise time Crawford had killed his first four victims.*

Her skin crawled and her heart raced even faster. He couldn't have found her already. He couldn't have. It'd been only ten days…

She firmly gripped her weapon, swiped back the covers and then crept silently in the dark. Scraping her back against the wall, she inched down the hallway, not daring to turn on her flashlight. The house had to appear unchanged from outside. Otherwise, whoever was out there would know she was inside. *Keep them guessing, Maggie.*

She scanned ceiling to floor. *Second bedroom… clear.* She skirted the landscape painting of the Louisiana bayou at sunset, and then moved on, the rough wall snagging her blouse at her back, abrading her skin. *Bathroom…clear.* Moving again, she listened intently for the slightest creak or groan, for any sense of movement or odd sound.

Nothing. She checked the windows then the front door, avoiding the peephole. As a profiler, she'd read way too many reports of people checking peeps and meeting with a bullet or a rammed sharp object. Instead she peeked out at the edge of the window beside the door, through the tiny gap between window casing and miniblind. *Nothing.*

No one standing on her porch. No light or darkness rupturing the soft amber rays and shadows cast by the streetlamp. No extra car at the curb or vehicle out of place. Nothing as it hadn't been for the past nine nights.

Stretching, she clasped a small mirror from a table beside the sofa and lifted it at an angle near the window to view the running length of the porch. *Rocker... unmoved. Planter...unmoved. Nothing at waist level obstructing her view.* Her hand not quite steady, she tilted the mirror down to reflect the porch floor and stilled.

What was that?

A dark clump lay on the welcome mat in front of the door. Straining, she made out the shape.

A black rose.

Her heart stopped then shot off like a launched rocket, shoving adrenaline through her veins that gushed and pounded in her ears. She jerked away from the window, fear churning in her stomach, turning the taste in her mouth bitter.

Her cell phone vibrated in its case clipped at her waist. She didn't recognize the number, let it go to voice mail, then checked the message.

"You can run. You cannot hide."

A distinct click ended the call.

He'd found her.

Maggie Mason had gotten careless.

Her running again hadn't surprised him. Without intercession, she'd already have been nailed. Neglecting to change phones before arriving in her new location... well, that was a rookie mistake she'd regret—and one he hadn't failed to exploit. Why a nonrookie of her caliber had made that mistake intrigued him. She was a formidable adversary and a beautiful woman. The sales clerk remembered her. They always remembered beautiful women. Getting her new number had been sinfully easy. He hadn't needed to go that route, of course, but doing so gave him more options in his backup plans. He'd long ago learned the value of backup plans.

The temperature had dropped at least twenty degrees since nightfall, into the teens. His arms and legs long since numb, he tucked his phone back in his pocket then slid the zipper and risked bending sideward from the tree just far enough to glance across the street. By now she'd surely seen the gift he'd left on her front porch.

His nose was running. He swiped at it, mask to sleeve, not daring to sniff. Her neighbor two doors down had a dog. The last thing he needed was for the mutt to start barking and rouse the whole neighborhood. The cold had frozen his skin and the swipe set it to burning. The wind sliced right through him, making his eyes water and the cold seep straight into his bones, but the prospect of winning his prize kept him plenty warm.

He waited fifteen minutes. Saw no signs of her stirring inside the house. No light came on, no movement at the windows, no lifting of the garage door signaling her getting into her car and beating a hasty retreat.

Staying put, eh?

Not a smart move for a very smart woman. But with the way this operation had developed, a lucky break for him.

He checked the street—silent and still—then peered through the darkness and stubbed branches of trees that had lost too many leaves for his liking. Still no movement in the house.

Well, if she wasn't coming out to her car so he could

handle this in her garage, that left him no choice but to go in.

He crouched low and slithered down the shrubs, pausing near a large oak. Its low-slung limb bent double, nearly scraping the ground. It would give him cover to get closer to the house before exposing himself out in the open. The woman was a marksman. He couldn't afford to forget that.

Scrape.

Metal. Where had the scraping noise come from? Echoing through the trees, he couldn't peg the source, but instinct told him it was from her house. He stilled. Shallowed his breath behind the black stocking mask that left open only slits for his mouth and eyes. Ran a visual perimeter scan, checking her neighbors, but saw nothing amiss. Wind brushing a tree limb against a metal gutter? *Likely.* The mutt down the street hadn't alerted. Had to be something typical or he'd be yelping. Idiot dog had barked at his own shadow most of last night during his reconnaissance here. His owner had come outside twice to check things out. Fortunately, he never intended to act last night. But tonight he didn't want anyone seeing or hearing anything. When they found her body, he wanted nothing reported—just the entire neighborhood to be rocked and in total shock that while they'd slept, a murder had occurred right under their noses.

He took a step away from the tree, tripped over an exposed root. Pain shot through his frozen toes and he clenched his teeth and looked down to his neon blue shoe.

She'd pay for that.

Scrape.

There it was again. Distinct—and definitely metal.

She'd never just come out. Maggie Mason was far too clever for that. She'd lay some kind of trap for him going in. Unfortunately, in her line of work, she'd been exposed to many possibilities from which to choose. He shifted his vantage point, moving farther down the fence to get a better view of the backyard. The row of squat bushes along the back of the house shimmered. *Wind?* He scanned the clapboard. Solid. No door. Probably a raccoon. He'd spotted two last night, one in her yard, one next door. He waited a full minute...then another, but the metal scraping didn't repeat a third time.

He crept silently down the fence, tree to tree, crossing the outer edge of the backyard to the far side of the lot, then worked his way up the fence on the side of the house. The back door was metal.

His stomach sank. Had she slipped past him? No. No way. Her car hadn't moved—he'd had his eye on the garage door the entire time. She couldn't very well walk out of here in the dead of night.

Moving stealthily, bush to tree to bush, he made his way closer to the door. She was in there. She had to be in there.

The only way Maggie Mason would be leaving this house was toes-up in a body bag.

TWO

Facedown in the dirt behind the bushes, Maggie watched him make his way around the perimeter of the yard until the house blocked him from sight. He was going for the door. She released the heavy string tied to the back screen door that she'd tugged to create the scraping sound, and then ran under the cover of the trees. Charging the stacked wood, she climbed, hopped the fence and then ran full out, cutting across lawns and between homes, not daring to pause to glance back.

Three blocks over, she spotted the junkyard. Her lungs burned, threatening to explode, and her leg, though stronger, was still weak from the Utah incident, and it throbbed. Snagging the key from under the fender of a clunker, she hopped in and then cranked the engine. Was he already following her?

Scared to death, she dumped her emergency bag into the passenger's seat, her weapon within reach on the console, and then cut across the parking lot to the T-street intersection. Scanning, she spotted no other cars, no one walking. Easing on the gas to minimize spewing gravel and leaving a calling card on the direction she was taking, she pulled out and reported a prowler to the local police, then followed the map she'd committed to memory to hit Highway 51 South.

* * *

All the way to Macon, she kept one eye firmly on the rearview, but spotted no signs of him behind her. Right before the exit, she retrieved an unused prepaid cell from her emergency pack and called in. "This is Sparrow," she said and then went through the positive identification ritual with an unidentified woman whose voice she didn't recognize. "Tell Henry I'm on my way and let the task force know."

"Already? It hasn't even been two weeks this time."

Like she didn't know that? "Already." Seeing the neon sign, she ended the call then pulled into the all-night gas station the agency had arranged. The man on duty watched her pull in and frowned. Word had already come down to him from on high.

She parked the clunker away from the street and grabbed her bag.

"He found you."

"Yeah." She dropped a key to the clunker in Henry's hand. "And he could be on my heels, so..."

"Key's on the board." Henry nodded to the near wall inside. "Red Honda out back."

"Thanks, Henry."

"I'm so sorry, Sparrow."

"Yeah." She nodded. "Me, too." She moved quickly inside, grabbed the key and then walked straight through to the back door. The red Honda was parked nose-out next to the building in deep shadows. She jumped inside, locked the doors, pulled on a wig that made her a brunette and then headed back down 51 South.

The agency assisted her, planting cars and other things she needed along her path, but neither it nor its field agents could protect her. Oh, the task force did what it could, but if it couldn't catch Crawford for the killings, it couldn't prevent him from killing her. The team knew it. The agency knew it. She knew it. *What are you going to do, Maggie?*

What was she going to do? He'd not only found her, but he'd meant to kill her. Tonight. Crawford had tired of the cat-and-mouse game, and he was done playing. Now he wanted her dead and out of the way.

Had he just been playing with her all this time? Could he have killed her at any time he wanted?

The more she thought about it, the more she believed that's exactly what he'd been doing. She couldn't protect herself. And now that he had decided to end the game, she had two choices: One. Get help. Two. Die.

She didn't want to die.

Glancing at the amber dash clock, she fretted over her choices. And that this attack signaled he was itching to kill again. She and her death didn't count. He was ready to resume killing his regular victims. She was just an obstacle he wanted out of his way for fear she'd catch him. Yet she had kept him otherwise occupied longer than anyone believed she could. Three years, nearly four. Still, that he was eager to resume his killing spree made her sick inside. He had a two-week span at Christmas every year that set everyone at the agency on edge, worrying that he would kill, shocked and grateful when he didn't. Why he always murdered his victims during those two specific weeks remained a mystery, though Maggie suspicioned they had something to do with his mother. What exactly, she didn't know. But tenuous threads led to her.

Maggie glanced at her watch. Nearly 1:00 a.m. She needed a sounding board. She needed Ian. Fishing her phone from her bag, she punched the second number on speed dial.

On the third ring, a drowsy Ian answered. "Crane."

The urge to cry slammed into Maggie. She didn't dare to give in to it. "Ian, it's me."

"Maggie?" Surprise flooded his voice. "Are you okay?"

"So far." She swallowed hard, speeding up to pass a slow-moving SUV in the left lane. In bits and spurts, she shared what had happened, and then said, "I thought I could do it, Ian. But I can't. This time, I had no idea he was even close until I saw the rose on the porch." She couldn't count a weird feeling something was wrong. That wasn't enough to qualify. Bitterness set in. "I should go back and shoot him." She considered it.

"He was going to kill me. He's already killed four women. I love life and preserve it whenever possible, but it's him or me, and I can't run anymore." Her chin quivered. She clamped it.

"You saw him?" Ian asked, shocked. "He was that close?"

"It was too dark to see his face, but it was Crawford. He was going into my house when I got away. Tonight was going to be the night."

Ian sucked in a sharp breath. "Why didn't you shoot him?"

She swallowed hard. "You know why." The same God that made her made Crawford. She'd do it if she had to, but she prayed every day of her life that she wouldn't have to take that step. It'd change her forever, and oh, but she feared that change.

"I do." He sighed. "But you better accept that you might not be able to escape."

"If I can't, then I'll do what I have to do."

"Are you safe now?"

"I think so." Instinctively, she checked the rearview

mirror but didn't see anyone tagging her in the light traffic. "I've switched cars twice since escaping."

"Maggie, him getting this close this fast...it's time to accept help. He will kill you."

"I know. I think he's been playing me, letting me think I was staying ahead of him when he's known my every move. How, I have no idea. But it's a bad sign." A chill had her skin crawling. "He's ready to move on."

"You think he'll stop coming after you?"

"No." She didn't. "I think he's eager to kill me so he can resume his regular murders unhampered." *You can run. You cannot hide.* His words echoed through her mind. "It's time."

"Time for what?"

"For him to kill again." Her breath stuttered. "He's been dormant while he's been occupied with me—at least, as far as we can tell. But if he repeats past patterns, before the end of December, he'll kill again." All four murders had been a week either side of Christmas.

"That's all the more reason to come home and let me help. Maybe if he can't get to you, then whomever he's targeted to be this Christmas's victim will survive."

That thought struck home. Yet another countered it. "To get to me, he'll kill everyone around me." Ian. Paul and Della. Uncle Warny. Probably even Jake, Paul's Rottweiler.

"He could try," Ian conceded. "But we're all trained and we've dealt with killers before. All of us, Maggie. Paul and Della, Madison and Grant and Jimmy." He reeled off the names of everyone on the staff at Lost, Inc. "I don't know about Mrs. Renault, but frankly, I wouldn't test her. The woman has a steel backbone and titanium nerves."

She did. Madison's assistant was more than capable of handling herself. She'd had to be. Her husband had been the commander of the base until his death, which meant she'd had to fend for herself against some very real enemies who considered the commander's wife a plum target. Still, this wasn't a garden-variety killer. This was Crawford. It was nearly impossible to defend against Crawford. "No one has faced a killer like him, Ian."

"We've faced ones a lot like him."

By the tone of Ian's voice, she knew he wasn't softening his words for her sake or straying from the truth. Paul had never told her that. Common sense said in their military experience, Paul and those at Lost, Inc., went after terrorists, but a serial killer of Crawford's caliber? "Really?"

"We got a mix of sociopaths and psychopaths along with the brainwashed and fanatics, Maggie. But it's a moot point anyway. We're your last resort."

Last resort. The very words she'd thought herself to signal that her survival depended on accepting outside help. She wrestled the pros and cons and ended up staring into the bleak depths of fact: on her own, she was as good as dead. *Last resort.* It had to be a sign.

Her mind settled. "I'm driving straight through. Don't call Paul. He'll freak out until I walk through the door. Let him and Della have their trip to her step-grandmother's."

Ian didn't acknowledge her response, likely because he intended to call Paul anyway, but he did ask a question. "How did Crawford find you?"

"I don't know." She'd been so careful. So methodical and cautious in preparing the house, stacking the wood to climb the fence, stashing her backup vehicles—everything. Her palm went damp and the phone grew slick. *The phone.* Surprise streaked through her chest. "Oh, Ian. It's my fault."

"Why?"

"I bought the new phones at the same time I got to my new house." He'd been in hot pursuit of her when she'd left her last one, and rather than buying multiple phones at different locations, she'd cut down on stops by buying several phones at once. It'd been a busy store, but apparently not busy enough that the clerk had forgotten her.

He groaned. "Take out the battery."

Even turned off, a phone with a battery in it could be tracked. "I know." *Shouldn't have cut corners. Should have made the stops.* She rapped the heel of her hand on the steering wheel.

"Do it now, Maggie—and call me as soon as you can after you replace it."

"I will." She ended the call, then unsnapped the back and removed the battery. Likely Crawford knew exactly where she was until the moment the battery hit the console. "Stupid mistake." Cracking the heel of her hand against the steering wheel, she said it again. Twice.

Spotting a blue truck behind her, she punched the gas pedal and sped up, eager to put as much distance as possible between her and where she'd been when she'd disabled the phone.

Her eyes gritty and burning, she checked the highway sign. Still north of Nashville and still pitch-dark. Oh, but she looked forward to dawn.

A few miles later, she checked the dash clock—after three in the morning. It felt like a lifetime since the doorbell had awakened her. She was exhausted and yet running on so much adrenaline, even if she were in a position to sleep, she wouldn't be able to do it. The blue truck she'd been watching moved up, now one car behind her. Had there been a blue truck in her neighborhood?

She mentally went down the block for the hundredth time, but she couldn't recall one. Still, the truck's sole occupant—gauging by height in the driver's seat, a man—hung close, watching her.

No one could positively identify Crawford. She had never seen his face, either—he'd always worn a mask, just as he had in her backyard earlier that night. Was he driving the truck? Or maybe the driver was some unsuspecting minion he'd hired? The man could be anyone. Worse, anyone could be Gary Crawford.

She slowed down, trying to nudge him into passing her. He hesitated then pulled alongside and stared at her through the window, his face lit up by his eerie green dash lights. She didn't recognize him. Couldn't recall running into him at a gas station or the grocery store or anywhere else. Henry might have alerted the bureau she'd picked up the car. The driver could be one of theirs, but he didn't signal he was an agent riding shotgun for added protection. Was he Crawford? Her skin crawled. *Stop it, Maggie.*

She did need to stop it. Things were bad enough. The man could be an unrelated outsider, but he kept pace and stared too hard for too long to be up to anything but no good. Maybe a guy bent on preying on a woman traveling alone in the wee hours before dawn.

Unfortunately, she'd run into that kind of thing enough times to have lost count.

If he were Crawford, odds favored him pulling alongside her just long enough to fire a bullet into her car. When Crawford was done with the game, he was done. That left the second option—a predator seeking prey. She knew how to deal with predators. Reaching to the console, she lifted her weapon and propped it on her hand gripping the steering wheel. The steel glinted in her amber dash lights.

Shock widened the truck driver's eyes. He floored his accelerator. The engine whined, kicked in. The truck belched black smoke, and he sped off into the night.

Shaking and clammy, fighting that same need to scrub herself from head to toe she always felt on a close call with Crawford, she put the gun back down on the console. Soon she'd be in Nashville. The sun would be up; she'd stop and get a phone, and then call Ian.

She hated to admit, even to herself, just how badly she needed to hear his voice.

Where was Maggie's last note?

Ian felt certain he'd left it on the table next to his easy chair. He'd been reading it before Talbot and Dayton came over to watch the game. But he couldn't find it now.

Returning to the kitchen, he paced the hardwood floor between it and the den, watching the clock just as he'd been watching it for the past three hours, waiting for Maggie to call back. Hoping Crawford wasn't following her. That he hadn't found her through her phone locator. That he wasn't ten minutes behind her on the highway.

He poured himself yet another cup of coffee and fought his conscience. The battle raged. Torn between calling and not calling Paul. Paul should know. He really should know…

But she'd specifically told Ian not to call her brother. Specifically.

You've got to do something.

Ian paused, leaned against the breakfast bar. Do something. Like what?

Get her home faster and out of Crawford's reach.

He could do that. General Talbot and Colonel Dayton were in Nashville. He could have her meet them at the airport. They'd bring her home.

They're going to blame someone for the security breach.

They were. But Maggie hadn't been in North Bay. She couldn't be a target for leaking word about the Nest. She didn't even know the secret facility existed.

He paced some more, arguing both sides with himself, and got nowhere. Finally, he gave in and called Paul. If he did ask Talbot and Dayton for help, he couldn't do it without Paul's blessing. With his connections, he could know reasons for doing it or, equally important, for not doing it. Stretching, Ian grabbed the phone.

"Ian, it's me."

"Thank heaven." The relief in his voice turned hard. "It's nearly 7:00, Maggie. I expected you to call hours ago. The things I've been seeing in my head—"

Sitting in the Walmart parking lot, she glanced in the rearview and didn't immediately recognize the woman reflected in the mirror as herself. Short brown wig, sunglasses and bright red lipstick. *Ugh!* "Sorry. I just got the new phone." Not that changing phones would stop Crawford. It hadn't stopped him so far. Somehow he still managed to track her. *How? An agency leak? A leak on her military consults?* The entire task force had tried to find out, but no one had found a thing... yet. TV shows made it all look so simple, but in real life, everything didn't wrap up all nice and neat, tied with a pretty bow. More's the pity.

"Are you all right? Being followed?"

"Tired but fine, and I haven't picked up on anyone following me."

"Where are you?"

She sipped from a large cup of steaming-hot coffee before answering. "About an hour out of Nashville." Clarkston, Tennessee, actually, but it was safest not to be too specific. "I'm driving straight through, so I should be in about 4:00 this afternoon. Maybe a little later if I get too tired." She was eager to get there, but not eager enough to endanger others on the road.

"You can't make that drive on no sleep."

"He won't be far behind me, Ian. I don't have any choice."

"Actually, you do. Just get to the Nashville airport, last depot in the terminal."

"I can't fly. He'll be watching, and even if he doesn't make the plane and jeopardize the other passengers, he'll be waiting when I step off. I don't know how he manages, but I've tried that before, and it just doesn't—"

"You're taking a private flight home on a military plane. My old commander, General Talbot, and his assistant, Colonel Dayton, have been in Nashville for a summit. They're ready to head back, just holding the flight until you get there."

Relief washed through her and she smiled. "You've been busy."

"If you recall, Paul, Della and Madison once worked for them, too."

"Yes, but they didn't call the general, did they? My guess is Mrs. Renault did." Madison's assistant. The widow of the man General Talbot replaced.

"Talbot wouldn't dream of refusing her anything."

Maggie's mind might be numb, but Ian was thinking. *Clever.* "He's been in love with her for years—well, since she's been widowed." He'd lost his own wife a decade ago.

"I've heard that, too," Ian agreed. "Which is why I suggested she be the one to call him."

Maggie laughed. "You are sly, Ian Crane. I can't say I've noticed that about you before, but I appreciate it now." She got back on the interstate and headed to Nashville. "Do you have net access? I need to give you my new number."

"This one isn't it?"

"No, I'll ditch this phone as soon as we hang up. You know where I'll be leaving the number." Their email drafts account. It was their strongest secure communication link. "When you call me back, use a throwaway phone. If Crawford found me through my phone once, he can do it again—and he'll know who I've talked with, too."

"Has he traced your calls before?"

"Regularly." She blended into traffic and set the cruise control.

"That's no small thing, Maggie. How does he get access?"

"If I knew the answer to that, I'd find him long before he got close to me." The wig itched. She tried to ignore it. Took another sip of coffee.

"Paul doesn't know about Crawford tracing your calls, does he?"

He'd lose his mind worrying about her. "No, he doesn't." She put her cup back into its holder. "So let me guess. You held out until 5:00, then called him, right?"

Silence.

He'd called Paul, all right. The lack of an immediate denial proved it. "Ian?"

His sigh crackled static. "I held out until 5:15."

She smiled again, checked her mirrors. "I love it that you're predictable." She did. It made her feel secure, steady, to know what to expect. "Did he go postal?"

"Not postal, no. But he is plenty worried. He saved postal for when he called back."

"About what?"

"To tell me he was snowed in and couldn't get out. Then he definitely went postal."

Postal, and then some. Ian's tone made that evident. "I'm glad he's snowed in, and I hope it holds. I want him and Della safe." She shuddered. "This time Crawford got way too close, Ian. I'm still shaking inside. If I hadn't strung a string to the side door to open as a diversion, I seriously doubt I would have gotten past him this time."

"I know you. You prepared. I suspect it took everything you did to get past him, not one thing."

True. "Well, my everything really wasn't enough. I got lucky." Bumping the bushes. Crawford had stopped and stared right at her. She'd been terrified he was going to come right at her and she'd have to shoot him. Maybe she should have, but killing a human being—even one as twisted as Crawford—was reserved as a last resort.

Something had made him dismiss the shimmering bushes. What, she had no idea. "Things just as easily could have gone the other way." That truth left her chilled. She bumped the heater up a notch.

"Well, I'm glad they didn't."

So was she. Traffic was picking up. Getting close to Nashville, but also morning go-to-work traffic. "I'd better let you go so you can get ready for work. Will you be all right today, after me keeping you up all night?"

"I'm fine." He paused, and then added, "I don't sleep much anyway, and I thought we'd talk until you got on the plane."

He didn't want to break the connection. Her chest went warm in a way it shouldn't. The last thing either of them needed was a relationship complication. They were friends. Special friends—you can't trudge through grief and despair and terror as they had and not be— but just friends. "It's half an hour away."

"Yeah, it is."

Supporting her. She started to check her thoughts, but they tumbled out of her mouth anyway. "I appreciate you, Ian."

"Yeah? Then take pity and stop scaring me, Maggie."

The truth set in and her smile faded. "I expect it's going to get a lot scarier before it gets better. You know I'm right about that."

"Yes."

"He'll keep coming until one of us is dead."

"I know."

"Others could get hurt."

"Yes."

"You could get hurt. If you want to back off, I wouldn't blame you." If she could back off, she might.

"No way. I'm here for you."

"Ian, seriously." She lifted a hand from the steering wheel and flexed her stiff fingers. "I'm touched, but I don't want you to feel you have to put yourself in Crawford's line of fire. You don't." That's the last place she wanted anyone.

"Drop it, Maggie. You're there, I'm there, end of story."

Quite a distance to go for even a special friend. Was that a blessing or a curse? She couldn't be sure, but she prayed after all he'd been through with Beth, their friendship would be a blessing to him. Crawford was the curse.

He's going to kill you or make you kill him.

Her chest went tight. All her muscles contracted at once, and the urge to give in to despair or scream dueled inside her. She gave in to neither, and instead said, "We know how this is going to end. I wish... I hate..." She couldn't make herself say it. "Never mind."

"The idea of killing anyone?"

"Yes." She swallowed hard. "But he won't stop, and I don't want to die."

"I know." Ian sighed. "It's a hard road, but it will sort out. Sometimes we have to do things we don't want to do. We don't have to like them, but we do have to do them. You know that better than anyone."

Undercover, trapped in Crawford's cat-and-mouse maze for over three years, yes, she knew it. She moved over into the left lane, passed a green Avalon, then eased back into the right lane and tapped off her blinker with her pinky. "You know what scares me the most?"

"What?"

"It's shameful. I—I... No, I can't say it. I don't want you to know I'm that awful a person."

"You're a good person. Now tell me." He sniffed. "We talk freely, remember?"

She dropped her voice. "What scares me most is I want him dead. Not in jail. Not injured. Dead. I feel awful about that, but it's the only way I know he'll ever leave me alone and stop killing."

"It's hard to imagine you wouldn't want him dead. His death is your only shot for any kind of life, much less peace."

"But it's horrible to want anyone dead."

"Ah, faith. You're worried about the conflict between your beliefs and actions, and living with what you do that God won't approve, right?" He sighed. "I understand, but if you don't stop him, he will keep killing other people. In or out of jail, Gary Crawford is going to murder. Don't you think God considers that?"

"I'm betting my eternity on it. But still, Ian. Wanting someone to die? I'm judging. That's not God's way." Shame slithered over her. "He's got to be so disappointed in me."

"If He is, you're in line behind me. We're not on speaking terms, as you know. But I still expect He's proud of you. Pretty courageous, using yourself to draw Crawford's fire to keep him from killing others—especially after he nearly killed you." Ian paused, waiting and maybe hoping she'd deny it, but she couldn't. That's exactly what she'd been doing with this self-imposed exile. Finally, Ian went on. "God surely wants you safe. Self-defense is self-defense."

"I don't remember seeing that written behind 'Thou shall not kill.'"

"Oh, please. Don't tell me you think God expects you to stand still and let someone else kill you. There are plenty of instances where God created circumstances and conditions to protect His own on the battlefield. If this isn't a battle, I don't know what is."

She hadn't thought of her situation that way, but Ian was right. Four soldiers sounding like an army... "How do you know this is a situation where I'm supposed to battle and defend myself?" That had perplexed her for a long time and had been the focus of many prayers during this ordeal.

"I know because God loves you."

"But He loves Crawford, too." She was too tied up in knots for this conversation now.

"You're really muddled about this."

"I am. I'm having a hard, hard time with it, Ian."

"I wish I could be more reassuring. I do believe God understands, and if it's kill or be killed, He'll understand that, too."

"I hope so."

"Maybe when you get home, you can talk to the pastor. Surely he can walk you through it."

"I can't talk to him about this. It—it's horrifying to admit you want someone else dead."

"Crawford isn't just someone. He's a cold-blooded killer who's murdered four women and is bent on killing you so he can kill even more."

She shouldn't ask. Shouldn't, but she was going to do it. "Will you come with me—to talk to the pastor?"

"Oh, Maggie, don't ask me to do that." He groaned. "You know I don't go to church anymore."

He was still angry with God for not sparing Beth. Still outraged that while he was serving to protect, his own wife was murdered and God had let it happen. Disappointment rippled through her. She'd hoped... Never mind what she'd hoped. She had no business hoping that anyway. They were friends and neither of them could afford to forget it or to ever expect anything more. Between Beth and Crawford, it just couldn't happen. Not now, not ever. "You won't come with me, then?" Why had she asked that? What was wrong with her?

Fatigue. Had to be that she was so tired and scared and her defenses were down and her confidence at being able to protect herself lay tattered not on the floor but under it.

Ian blew out a sigh so strong she felt it on her end of the phone. "All right, I'll come with you."

She sank her teeth into her lower lip. "Thank you, Ian. Now get over to the store, get a throwaway phone and then call me back."

"I'm going, but we'll talk on the way."

Touched, Maggie repeated herself. Special man. Special friend. "I'm grateful for you, Ian."

"Only when you're getting your way."

"You think?"

"I know."

She laughed, lush and deep.

On his way to the store, he caught her up on all the latest news in North Bay, and on his way home, he shared all the latest news about Lost, Inc. Madison was on a Christmas cruise, Jimmy had flown to Bainbridge Island off the coast of Washington and Mrs. Renault was at a resort in the Carolinas until after New Year's Day. He expected they'd all head home to assist on the Crawford case.

Maggie hoped not. She whispered a quick prayer to keep them in place and listened to Ian talk about his agreeing to hold down the fort at the office this holiday season.

"So it's you and me."

"Until they can get back here, yes. Oh, and your uncle Warny."

Who was bat-blind, nearly as lame as Thunder, her favorite rescue horse at the ranch, and quick on the trigger anyway. Maybe coming home wasn't such a good idea. She'd have to watch over Uncle Warny, too…

Certainty filled her. Going home was important. She couldn't explain it, but she sensed it. Maybe it was a deep longing for home, or a divine nudging. Whatever it was, it was there and she would heed it and pray hard for the best.

From the sounds coming through the phone, Ian pulled the truck into the garage and closed the door while filling Maggie in on Madison's new love/hate relationship with Grant Deaver.

"I don't know him."

"He's a former OSI officer. Just separated from the military and Madison snagged him."

"Ah. Well, I'm glad someone's finally gotten her attention." Truthfully, getting it wasn't hard—Madison noticed everything and always had—it was keeping it.

"He's got her attention, all right. She doesn't trust him, but anytime the two of them are in the same room, sparks between them fly."

"That kind of attention's got to be making Madison crazy." Maggie had never known her to associate with people she couldn't trust. But chemistry on top of that? Definitely personal…and very interesting.

"Actually, I think she likes it. He's a challenge," Ian said then corrected himself. "Well, he's clearly crazy about her, so it isn't that he's a challenge, it's whether or not she should trust him that makes him challenging."

"Why shouldn't she trust him?"

"I told you he just left active duty. He was stationed at the base and there's been a bit of an incident. I can't get into details."

Madison had been a POW. Her military days weren't fond memories. "She's strong and smart. She'll work through it."

"She will," Ian said. "Not that I like seeing her off balance, but it's entertaining to watch. I've never seen her like this with anyone."

"I don't think I have, either." A green sedan passed another vehicle and two cars back tucked into Maggie's lane. From the tag, the same green sedan that had been parked nose-to-nose and three cars down the row from her at Walmart.

Ian talked on.

Maggie focused on the sedan. She passed a white Volvo, then sped up and passed a blue Ford.

The green sedan followed and kept pace.

"Ian," she interrupted. "I've picked up a tail. Green sedan." She reeled off the tag number from memory. "One person in the car. Male. About forty-five. Dark hair, sunglasses. Can't make out anything else."

"Where are you?"

"Coming up on the airport exit."

"Traffic heavy?"

"Not too bad."

"Floor it."

Maggie stomped the pedal, stayed in the center lane and honked at the car in front of her to move over.

The driver did, but glared at her. She pushed the pedal harder, wove lane to lane between cars.

The sedan did, too.

"He's definitely following me." She stayed in the center lane, spotted the sign—a quarter mile to the airport exit. Her nerves drummed a wicked beat. She was going way too fast. Way too fast for him to expect her to exit. She jerked the wheel to the left, passed a pickup and then whipped in too close in front of an eighteen-wheeler. He slammed on his brakes. At the last minute, she hit the exit ramp, her brakes churning smoke the entire way down the circular off-ramp.

The truck blocked the sedan. He couldn't see her or make the exit. That could buy her a few minutes. Not many, but a few.

"You okay?" Ian sounded worried, fearful.

"So far. He couldn't turn. But I don't know how far it is to the next exit. I might have a minute, maybe a little more. I just don't know."

"Was the guy Crawford?"

"I don't know. I've never seen his face—just the mask. But he was definitely tagging me."

"Get to the cargo terminal, Maggie."

She sped the entire way, stuffed her weapon into her bag, abandoned the car in short-term parking and then ran full out the entire way into the terminal.

Colonel Dayton stood in uniform just inside, waiting for her. His sunglasses shaded his eyes. He whipped them off. "You all right, Maggie?"

A stitch in her side, she pressed a hand over it. "He's right on my heels."

"Let's move." He reached for her bag. "I thought you were blonde."

"I am." She hesitated, still breathless. "I'm also armed."

He smiled. "I'd be surprised if you weren't." He motioned with his fingers to pass the bag. "I'm already cleared."

Maggie half tossed it to him. "Hurry."

Within minutes they were on the C-17 and Colonel Dayton was passing her over to General Talbot.

Tall and lean, he was a little grayer than she recalled but still had the same kind eyes. She'd first met the base commander years ago when everyone had gathered at Beth and Ian's for a Super Bowl party, and he always attended community events. Maggie shook his hand. "It's good to see you, General." She smiled. "Thanks for rescuing me."

"Mrs. Renault said it was a matter of life and death."

"I'm sorry to say, she's right."

"Gary Crawford?" His graying brows lifted high on his forehead.

She nodded, not at all surprised he knew. After Utah, everyone did. That story was too big to be suppressed, and the media had had a field day with it for weeks. So the general clearly hadn't pressed Mrs. Renault for an explanation and Mrs. Renault clearly hadn't offered him one. Interesting. Why hadn't he pressed her? Odd. But then, maybe not so odd. Few pressed Mrs. Renault. She had an impeccable reputation and a very long history with these people.

Colonel Dayton stowed Maggie's bag in the overhead compartment next to one already there. "I can't believe Crawford hasn't been caught. He's been after you—how long?"

"Nearly four years." She could tell him down to the minute, but being specific made others uncomfortable.

The general frowned. "Sooner or later, he'll slip up. They always do." He pointed to a seat. "Buckle up and let's get out of here before he thinks to take out the plane."

She sat down and buckled up. "He'd never expect me

to be on a military flight. I've totally avoided planes since a little incident in El Paso."

"Why?" The general buckled in. "Seems it'd be the most efficient way to move long distances quickly and get lost."

She smoothed her hair back from her face. "He threatened to take hostages and kill a passenger a minute until I turned myself in to him. We got lucky that time. Trying it again knowing what he'd do…it's just not right."

Admiration lit in his eyes. "War makes for hard decisions we'd rather not have to make."

"Yes, it does." She stifled a yawn behind her hand. "Sorry. I haven't slept in a couple days. It's always like that when I move."

"You move a lot, don't you?"

"Unfortunately." He seemed gentle, which seemed at odds with his position. But maybe because of his position he could afford to be gentle.

"Are you hungry?" Dayton asked.

Her stomach hadn't stopped shaking. Until it did, she'd be crazy to mix flying and putting anything in it. "Not really."

"Rest then," the general said. "You'll feel better after a nap."

"Thank you. I really appreciate this."

The general nodded, opened a file and began reading.

The minute the plane lifted off, Maggie settled back and closed her eyes, sleeping soundly for the first time in a week.

The next thing she knew, someone was shaking her shoulder. "Miss Mason?" Another gentle shake. "Maggie?"

She startled awake, grabbed for the hand.

"It's okay. You're safe."

Wild-eyed, her heart racing, she struggled to focus and saw Colonel Dayton's stern, tanned face. Her hand went to her chest. "Sorry."

His voice gentled. "I'm used to it. Happens a lot in those returning from combat zones."

She nodded. "I guess it is similar…except I'm nearly sure my combat zone will be following me home."

"If we can help…" the general started.

"Thank you." She straightened. They were on the ground. The plane had landed, taxied and stopped near the terminal.

Dayton frowned. "I hated to wake you, but there's a man pounding the ramp, eager to see you."

She glanced out the window and saw Ian. "How did he get out there?"

"I took care of that." The general smiled. "Seems like a little thing, but I know it's not—not to him, and I suspect, not to you."

Touched by his thoughtfulness, Maggie smiled. "Thank you, General."

Colonel Dayton stretched into the overhead and grabbed her bag. He unzipped a side pocket in her bag and removed her weapon. "You can get this back on the other side of the terminal."

She nodded.

He grabbed the zipper on the second bag and tugged. Maggie spotted something bright blue. He dropped the gun inside and closed the zipper.

Unbuckling, she stood up and covertly stretched, stiff from head to toe.

General Talbot reached for the bag with her weapon. "Best let me carry that."

"Yes, sir." Dayton passed it to him.

"Ready, Maggie?" the general asked.

She smiled. "Ready." She nodded and sized up Dayton yet again. He seemed uptight and proper, all business. Not like the type of man who'd ever wear aquatic neon blue shoes.

THREE

"Ian." Maggie ran into his open arms, sagged against him, relieved to finally be in a place she felt safe and secure. "I can't believe I'm really here."

He let out a sigh of pure relief. "Me, either. The elephant's off my chest and I can breathe again."

She pulled back, smiled at him. He looked the same. Still tall and fit and handsome, and dressed in khaki slacks and a cream-colored fleece-lined jacket that fit him and his personality. His face was tanned, a little leaner and more honed, but his eyes were still that fascinating blue and, if a little duller for the pain he'd endured, the sparkle she'd seen when they first met still shone in them. "You look…terrific."

He smiled. "I'd say you do, too, but I hate the wig and you've lost too much weight. Your uncle Warny is going to chew on you for that."

She laughed. "I can't say I care for the wig, either, and you know I always drop ten pounds when I have to move more than once in a short time." She shrugged. "You do what you have to do when things are as they are, but you also pay a price."

Dayton cleared his throat. "I'll meet you on the other side with your package." He nodded toward the terminal.

Ian and he shook hands. "Thanks a lot for bringing her home."

While Maggie thanked the general, Dayton lowered his voice to talk to Ian, but Maggie still caught his words. "Stay on your toes. Paul, too. A man driving the vehicle Maggie identified as the one following her hit the terminal not five minutes behind her. The FBI suspects Crawford hired him to tag her and refused to let us intercept him. I guess they're hoping he'll lead them to Crawford. You know he'll beeline it down here."

Keeping the news that Paul was away to himself, Ian sobered. "We'll be ready."

"She's exhibiting symptoms of PTSD," Dayton added, making no attempt to shield his voice from her. "You might watch that, too."

Ian nodded, looked over at her. She gave him a shaky smile. "I'm okay. Really. I just haven't slept much in a while."

"Well, let's get you home and remedy that." Ian guided her through the terminal. The general passed the bag off to Dayton, who followed her and Ian outside.

He transferred the weapon. "There you go."

She looked up at him and smiled. "Thank you again—for everything, Colonel." It felt kind of nice to have someone concerned about her when it wasn't a blood or friendship obligation. She'd forgotten how that felt.

"Sure thing. Give Paul my regards."

Something in his tone rang insincere and sent a chill through her. She brushed it off, blamed it on exhaustion. The man had been nothing but good and kind to her.

Ian led the way to his Ford Expedition. It was white, trimmed in gold around the fenders and bottom, and was even greater-looking than in the photos. He opened the passenger door.

Maggie stepped onto the running board and then slid into the creamy leather seat. Ian walked around to the driver's side and got inside. "Nice," she told him. "The photos didn't do it justice." She inhaled. "Don't you love that new-car smell?"

He keyed the engine. "It's more vehicle than I need most of the time, but it's versatile. I'm enjoying it."

She smiled. Ian Crane was an SUV nut. A really picky one, and she had the email drafts of his notes and photos to prove it. He'd shopped for months, picking out this vehicle, playing with options until he'd found exactly what he wanted. "Right."

He grinned. "Okay, I love it."

"Better." Honesty was essential. She bared her soul to this man, and she couldn't do that unless he was just as honest with her. Lowering her sunglasses from their perch atop her head, she seated them on her nose to shade her eyes. The sun was blinding.

They left short-term parking and headed north of town, toward the ranch. It was hard to believe—to even imagine—but in half an hour, she'd be home. *Home...*

Ian glanced her way. "How long do you think you've got before Crawford shows up?"

Didn't she wish she knew? "I hope a good while. North Bay is the last place he'd expect me to come. I haven't dared to even visit since Utah." When he'd blown up her car and nearly killed Paul and her, she'd decided the risks to others were too great. She couldn't lead him to Paul's doorstep.

"I know and I'm sure he does, too." Ian cast her a worried, sidelong look. "But is it the first place he'll look?"

Had he done so before? A shiver coursed through her. "I don't know. He had to know I was on that plane."

"Possible, but doubtful. The military wouldn't disclose it. But someone who saw you in the terminal could." Ian shifted on his seat. "You should be okay at the ranch. Paul and your uncle Warny beefed up security during the ordeal with Della's stalker."

"Seriously? I didn't think that was possible."

"Every inch of the entire ranch is now under camera surveillance." He adjusted the heater.

Paul was a security specialist. He took the skills he'd acquired while in Special Operations and expanded them when he'd left the military. Honestly, after Utah, he'd gone a little security nuts, trying to entice her to come home and stay. "If he's added biometric-scanning to get from the living room to the kitchen, I'm going to say he's gone too far. This side of that, I'm good with all the help I can get."

Worry flashed through Ian's eyes. He reached over and clasped her hand.

She wasn't expecting it and his touch surprised her. But, oh, it felt good to have someone hold your hand when you were scared. She gave his fingers a gentle squeeze, rested their linked hands and laced fingers on his thigh. "Thank you, Ian."

"What for?"

A little choked up, she buried it and swallowed hard. Emotions were one thing she couldn't afford—and hadn't been able to afford for a long time now. They clouded judgment, muddying your thinking. They made you even more vulnerable, and those were dangerous luxuries. "Being there for me."

"That's a given. As much as you did for Beth...how could I not be there for you?" He grunted. "And for me.

Since Beth's death, I've been half out of my mind, trying to find out…" He stopped, sighed. "I don't know how I'd have gotten through these three years without you."

So he was doing this for Beth and because he felt he owed Maggie. Her heart sank, though it had no right to. He'd never led her to believe there was anything more between them—and there shouldn't be. In Crawford's eyes, that'd paint a bull's-eye on Ian's forehead.

"You really okay?" He stopped at a traffic light then headed north, away from town and toward the ranch.

"I'm fine." She forced herself to smile…and again questioned the wisdom of coming home. "It's just not the homecoming I've dreamed about with Paul not here."

"He'll get home as soon as the weather lets up and he can." Ian glanced over. "Until then, you're stuck with me." His eyes twinkled. "Lucky you."

"Yeah." She smiled. "Lucky me."

The reunion was sweet.

Uncle Warny sat in his usual chair, his glasses tucked into his red flannel shirt pocket, smiling at Maggie through red-rimmed, tear-blurred eyes with his arms stretched wide.

She flew into them, felt them close around her.

"Oh, Maggie girl, I'm so glad you're home safe." His huge body trembled.

"I missed you." She stroked his face.

"'Course you did. I'm a charming fellow."

She smiled. "I saw on the way in you've been exercising Thunder. He's moving a lot better." When she'd left here, he'd barely been able to move.

"We muddle along together. He likes his walks by 10

every morning or he stiffens up." Uncle Warny chuckled. "Me, too."

"He's your favorite."

"They're all my favorite, but Thunder's special." His eyes twinkled mischief. "Like Paul."

She leaned close. "Don't you tease me, old man. I'm your favorite, and you know it."

"Course you are, sweet pea."

"I'm sniffing blackmail fodder," Ian said, smiling. "Not telling Paul... It's going to cost you, Maggie."

"I'll pay, but I have to say I'm disappointed in you, Ian Crane. I can't believe you'd break my brother's heart. He needs to be *somebody's* favorite." She tried but couldn't quite get a teasing tone in her voice. Not when she'd felt that way her whole life. Their parents sure hadn't done much to make either of them feel loved. But Uncle Warny...he was their blessing.

"Della's got Paul covered now, Maggie girl." Uncle Warny sent her a satisfied look. "That woman's positively moonstruck over your brother." He rubbed his neck. "About time, eh?"

Past time. Way past time. "Glad to hear it, but it proves I need you more, so I'm your favorite." They'd competed in play forever, and she only realized then how much she'd missed it. That was the thing about being alone. There was nobody and nothing to keep you grounded. To Paul and Uncle Warny—to Ian to an extent—she mattered.

"Absolutely." Warny belly-laughed.

Maggie twitched her nose at him and snitched another hug. "It smells like heaven in here." She motioned for Jake, the black Rottweiler waiting patiently for his turn and her attention, and ruffled his scruff. "Hey, boy. I'm glad to see you, too." His tail wagged furiously fast, smacking the leg of her jeans. She scratched his ears and looked over at her uncle. "You learned how to cook?"

"Naw, Della packed the freezer with all kinds of stuff before she and Paul headed out to her stepgrandma's." He lifted a sheepish shoulder. "She worries about me." And that she did clearly pleased him. "This one is roast, rosemary potatoes and glazed baby carrots—but it won't be ready for an hour and fifteen minutes. Then I have a peach pie to put in the oven."

"She made pie, too?" Maggie smiled. She'd talked to Della many times, and Paul being happy told her all she really needed to know, but that she'd opened her heart to their uncle, too...well, Della Jackson's stock rose from higher to highest in Maggie's book.

"Yep, a couple of 'em. She sure can cook." Warny looked at Maggie's eyes, homing in on the dark circles. "Have a nap, or go get your feet in the grass." He glanced over at Ian. "She ain't gonna feel like she's really home until she gets her own dirt under her feet."

Ian smiled. "She's notorious for that."

She was? "Did Paul tell you that?" She hadn't told him.

"Madison via Mrs. Renault." Ian crossed his arms.

Madison did know Maggie well, but how had Mrs. Renault discovered that? What was Maggie thinking; Mrs. Renault knew everything about everyone. "Walk with me."

Warny sent him a sly nod to keep close watch. Ian nodded back. "A short walk, Maggie. You need to rest."

"I slept the entire flight." She urged him around the table and toward the back door. "Come on, Jake."

He jumped to his feet and, nails clicking on the tile floor, got there first and nosed the glass.

"Some things never change." Nose prints. Maggie

laughed. "Open it up, lazy bones," she told the dog. "You know how to do it."

Jake batted the doorknob, and then pushed the door open.

On the back porch, she ditched her shoes and took off down the steps and across the lawn in bare feet.

Ian caught up with her. "Madison meant that literally—your bare feet in the dirt? In December?"

"After being in Illinois, it feels warm here." Maggie smiled but there was sorrow in it. "It's grass, actually, not the dirt. It's the land I need to feel under my feet."

"It's home." He stuffed a hand into his slacks pocket.

"Yes." She laced their arms. "You ever go home?" He and Beth had been from Texas, a little town just outside of Corpus Christi.

"Home's not there anymore. Mom and Dad are gone now, and so is Beth. There's nothing left to go home to."

"Did you sell the place?" His family had a thousand acres of prime farmland. He was an only child, so she assumed it was his now.

"Leasing it out." He shrugged. "Truth is, I can't go there, Maggie. I tried once, right after I got out of the military, but there're too many memories."

Maggie clasped his hand. "I can see where that would be really hard. But sometimes remembering is all you've got. They're kind of still with you then, if only in your heart and mind." He, Beth and Maggie had shared so many moments that she'd held on to while on the run. Picnics, lazy days at the beach. Sometimes Maggie would bring a date, sometimes not. They were close in the way friends who are open and honest with each other are…and then Beth had been killed and Ian had come home to mourn. Maggie had mourned with him, and their friendship had grown stronger, their bond forged to a depth only shared grief can forge.

"Maybe one day that'll feel good. But it doesn't yet."

He didn't say it. He didn't have to. Maggie knew. After Beth's murder was solved, then maybe he'd want to remember. Until then it wasn't comforting, it was haunting. How she wished she could make that easier for him, but she couldn't. He had to come to terms with that and with his anger at God over it in his own time and in his own way. Yet she could be there for him. Listen. Support. Do the things those who shared grief do for each other. It didn't seem like enough, but it was all there was. "Things happen in their own time."

"Yeah."

They walked along the fence toward the creek. The air was nippy, but crisp and clean. And the soft sounds of crunching leaves and running water at the creek soothed her, a tranquil balm to her weary soul.

Ian plucked up a broken twig from the ground. "The truth is, I'm stuck."

"Stuck?"

He tried to smile but it didn't touch his eyes. "Never mind. With all you've got going on, now isn't the time. I was being selfish."

Walking alongside, she patted his forearm. "Friends don't wait for the right time. Too often there isn't one. They talk when the need arises."

He glanced over at her, then out to the trees. "You know, even when you couldn't be here, you've been my main supporter." He grinned. "Does that make sense?"

"Perfect sense." The cards and email drafts. "I feel the same way." A soft hoot floated on the breeze and she smiled over at him. "Look. An owl." She lifted her chin toward a tall oak. "These woods used to be full of them." She'd heard them mostly at night, but occasionally during the day. "I wonder if they still are."

"Warny would know."

He would. "Owls always sound lonely, don't they?"

"I hadn't thought about it. Don't hear many of them in town."

"So what has you stuck?"

"Not now. You're tired." He patted her arm, still looped with his. "Let's just walk."

"Not finding Beth's murderer yet?" Maggie speculated, ignoring him. Innately, she sensed what he most needed to talk through was what he was most reluctant to discuss. That was generally always Beth's murder.

"How do you do that?"

Logic, pure and simple. "It's a woman thing." She wrinkled her nose at him. "So am I right?"

"Yeah, that's it," he confessed. "I'm feeling pretty hopeless. I mean, I try to stay focused on things not happening in my time but in God's perfect time."

"I thought you didn't pray anymore."

"I don't. But that doesn't mean I don't believe in Him. I'm just ticked off and disappointed. He let me down."

"So you're angry with God."

"Furious." His eyes glittered. "Sometimes so furious I can barely breathe."

A common reaction to the murder of a loved one. Some worked through it, some stayed angry with God forever. Her chest tightened. The thought of Ian being lost like that, not having the comfort of faith to help him through this, hurt her. It would break Beth's heart, too. "I can see why you'd feel that way…for a time."

"It is what it is. Beth's dead. I'm not."

Survivor's guilt. *Wretched mess.* Later would be soon

enough to tackle the spiritual challenges. For now, Ian needed to vent. "So no new leads?"

He nodded that there hadn't been. "No. Nothing new for a full year."

No way could he keep the pain of that truth out of his voice. He didn't bother to try. Not with Maggie. She'd know anyway, so it was just as well. Still, it made her feel special that he'd be open with her. He wasn't that way with the team at Lost, Inc. Madison had told Maggie so a hundred times. "I've studied all the documents, Ian."

He shot her a stunned look. "All of them?"

She nodded, stepped around a stump and over its exposed roots.

"How did you get them?" Even he hadn't had access to everything.

"I could tell you but then I'd have to kill you." She gave him a toothy grin.

He dragged in a sharp breath. "You're still active." It wasn't a question and she didn't insult him by denying it. He stopped cold. "Maggie, tell me I'm wrong. Tell me you're not still active."

She shrugged.

"What are you doing?" The truth dawned in his eyes. "You have been Crawford bait. I suspected it when you didn't deny it, but I can't believe you're active and the agency has allowed it?" He dragged a hand through his hair. "Oh, good grief. They've had you undercover." A vein in his neck bulged and his face flamed red. "What are those fools thinking?"

To avoid confirming or denying, she bent and picked up a dried twig, slung it across the field between them and the edge of the woods toward the creek. "He hasn't killed anyone else."

"Because he's been laser-focused on killing you." Ian frowned. "Does Paul know this?"

"I'm not confirming anything, but if I were still active and undercover, no one could know. So of course Paul wouldn't know."

"Don't insult me. You're active and undercover. Of course you are. Why doesn't Paul know? He should know."

"He'd interfere. After Utah, he'd remove me from the situation if he had to go to the media and spill his guts to do it. He can't know anything, and you will not tell him."

She gave him *the* look, and he glared right back at her. "But, Maggie…"

She softened her voice. "You will not tell him, Ian. There are other lives at risk."

"Crawford's future victims." Ian's jaw clamped and he squeezed his eyes shut a long second. When he re-opened them, accusation burned in their depths. "You didn't just come home so we could help protect you."

"Actually I did. I can't handle him alone anymore." Had she ever been able to handle him, or had that been an illusion? Her uncertainty blew holes in her confidence.

"Don't lie to me."

"I don't lie, Ian Crane." The wind caught her hair. She swiped the long strands of it back from her face. Her nose was cold from the nip in the air, her fingertips, too, but the grass under her feet made up for it. "You know how these things work. It was job essential. And this is confidential—all of it, and I mean it, Ian. If you tell Paul a thing, I'm leaving, and I'll do the best I can on my own."

"He'll kill you." Ian cut to the chase.

"Paul won't kill me."

"Not Paul—though he'll likely want to. Crawford. You came home for help, but not to deter him from hunting for you. You expect him to come after you."

"I stayed away to protect my family. That's the whole truth." She lifted a hand. "It didn't work. By his own words, anytime Crawford loses me, he will come after Paul." She paused and let that fact settle in. "There's only one way I'll ever be free of him and know he isn't killing again." She let him see the truth in her eyes.

"Then why didn't you shoot him in your backyard in Illinois?"

"Spiritually, I couldn't justify it so long as I thought I could get away from him. When I picked up his tail on the way to the airport, I had to accept that I couldn't." Acceptance hadn't come easily, and it wasn't painless. But she'd made peace with it.

"So you came here—" The truth dawned. Ian frowned, his shock in every tense line in his face. "Maggie, no. You can't mean—"

"I came home to confront him. On my turf. On my terms. With help I trust."

"I wanted you here, but I didn't know that you were set up as bait for him." Ian pressed a hand to his stomach as if he'd been sucker-punched to the gut. "The FBI sanctioned all of this?"

"After he found me in Illinois, well, we don't have a lot of options." She toed the grass, sought comfort in it. "Actually, we have one—this one. Crawford will kill again in the next two weeks, Ian. We're in his habitual countdown to Christmas. What else am I supposed to do?"

"You could really quit." He frowned. "Does Crawford know you're still active? Is that why he won't leave you alone?"

"I tried quitting. Publicly, I quit after Utah. I've been covert the entire time since I got off medical leave. But me quitting didn't stop him." Her bitterness about that put a sharp edge in her tone. "A few honchos at work, the task force members and now you are the only people who know I'm still FBI." She stared off into the deepening shadows in the woods. "From everything we can tell, Crawford bought into the public resignation due to the permanent damage to my leg—at the time, my recovery wasn't expected, if you recall."

"It's a miracle you've got as much mobility as you do."

"Almost a hundred percent. I've worked hard at it." She had been motivated and diligent.

"So Crawford thinks you're an artist and he's still after you."

She nodded. "There's been nothing to lead him to any other conclusion. Whether or not I was still an agent didn't matter to him. I got too close to him and he resents it. I was supposed to die in Utah and I had the audacity to live. He won't forgive me for that, or forget it."

"I know that's why he's still after you—because he failed to kill you." A wrinkle formed between Ian's eyebrows. "But why do you have to die before he can continue his killing spree?"

"Because he knows that with or without the FBI I'm going to try to stop him, and I see things others don't. That rattles him."

Ian dragged a hand through his hair and raised his voice. "So you're active, and when he isn't after you, you're still consulting with the task force and you're after him. Now you turn the tables and— Maggie, I urged you to come home, but I think I was wrong. In North Bay, you're a sitting duck. You'll be slivering your focus between keeping yourself safe and everyone else. You know everyone in town."

She did. Everyone who'd been here any length of time, and he had a point. But having help to face Crawford balanced the added risks. "I'm a sitting duck regardless of where I am. It's taken me a while to accept that, but it's true." She took in a deep breath. "Isn't being a sitting duck on my home ground, which has the best security money can buy, surrounded by people who love and help me, better than being a sitting duck on the run without security or help?"

Ian tossed the twig toward the woods. Jake took off like a shot after it. "I talked you into coming home, but it'd be better to be out of it altogether."

"Told you. I tried that." She slapped at her thigh. The muscle was stiffening up. "It didn't work, and I have the scars to prove it. So does Paul."

"I don't like any of this."

He wouldn't tell Paul, but he wasn't comfortable with the situation. How uncomfortable was he? Did she need to worry? "But you will support me, right?"

He glared at her, hesitated a long minute. "Yes, of course." He frowned and held it so she couldn't miss it. "But if you get yourself killed, I'm not forgiving you, Maggie, and I mean it. I'll throw rocks at your grave every day."

"That's fair." It'd probably be good aggression therapy for him. "I'll do my best not to put you through that." She looped their arms again and they walked back toward the house, Maggie leaning on him. All the activity and hours of driving, sitting had her knee stiff.

In the kitchen, Ian turned to her, his expression at

odds with his tone. "I'm going to head home. You be careful, and if you need me, call."

Maggie shoved her hair back from her shoulder. "Ian, don't you even think about leaving," she said before thinking. She'd just assumed with Paul away he would stay at the ranch with Uncle Warny in the barn apartment. "Um, we've got a Monopoly match set for after dinner and you're my best hope against the Monopoly King."

Ian chuckled. "Jake?"

"No, me," Warny grumbled. "Don't let these overalls fool you, son. I've got a knack when it comes to real estate."

Maggie guffawed. "I'll say. In four years, you've nearly tripled my holdings."

"Woulda done better if the market hadn't crashed and you hadn't made me help—"

"I'm not complaining." She cut him off. "I'm thrilled with what you've done." She turned to Ian. "You will stay, won't you, Ian?"

"Actually," Warny said, "I'd be obliged if you'd stay out here until Paul gets back...just in case."

Ian looked at Maggie.

She nodded. "Please. I know it's a huge inconvenience, but—"

"It's not inconvenient at all. I didn't want to shove my way in, but I wasn't going home, Maggie."

"What were you going to do?"

"Hang close and keep an eye out."

Watch over her.

"I'm glad to hear it," Warny said. "If that varmint Crawford comes sniffing around, between you, me, Jake and Maggie, he'll be sorry he did."

He just might. "Thank you, Ian." Maggie beamed, happy from the heart out. Finally, she was home.

"Uncle Warny," Maggie complained. "You can't buy Marvin Gardens. I always buy the yellow ones."

He glared at her over the tops of his glasses. "I can buy whatever's for sale…especially when you buy Park Place right out from under me."

Ian didn't dare laugh. "At least you two are landing on properties. All I seem to hit are railroads, utilities and that pay-taxes thing."

"No justice," Maggie said.

His gaze locked with Maggie's. She looked happy, and he felt less worried about her being here since Warny had walked him through the security system. If Crawford did show up, he wouldn't find attacking her easy—at least, not at the ranch. But that Ian worried about her, the way he worried about her, concerned him. It wasn't the worry of a friend but of a man who cared deeply for a special woman. He didn't have the right to worry about anyone like that.

Maggie rolled the dice and moved the thimble three places, to just visiting the jail. "Ian, you have to spend Christmas with us."

Warny winced. Ian understood why. Paul had invited Ian out every year since Beth's death. But he just couldn't celebrate holidays and there was little sense in dragging others down with him, so he opted to stay home alone. "I don't think—"

Maggie put a hand atop his on the table. "It's a great idea and it'll make me very happy. I've spent too many holidays alone, and I suspect you have, too. I want everyone important to me here. So, please, say yes. If not for yourself, then for me. Because I need it."

How did he refuse a frank plea like that? From anyone else, he'd have found a way. But from Maggie? He
couldn't do it, of course, yet he couldn't make himself
refuse her. "I'll think about it."

"Think all you like, my friend," Maggie said. "But
Christmas Day, when the turkey hits the table, your
backside better be in that seat or I'm going to cry my
eyes out because it's not." She rarely cried, but the
threat was extremely effective with Paul, Uncle Warny
and Ian. None of them knew what to do with a crying
woman but were wise enough to want to avoid one.
She blew out a sigh. "First time I'm home for Christmas in four years, and you'll make me cry all day. I
can't believe it."

Ian frowned at her. "That's blackmail, Maggie."

She walked her glass to the sink, filled it with tap
water and then took a long drink. "Yep, sure is."

He looked at Warny for reinforcement, but got a
grunt. "Don't look at me. You ever seen her cry? I seen
it once or twice, though it's been a spell. I still remember it and I'm telling you straight-out, I can't handle
it. Never could." Warny let out a sigh that heaved his
shoulders. "It's pretty bad, son. Probably easier on you
to just show up." He scratched at the back of his neck.
"Definitely easier on me."

Maggie brushed a hand across her mouth to hide a
smile. "Paul and Della want a happy Christmas, too."

"You're dragging them into this?"

"Do I need to?"

She had him. Either he capitulated or all of them
would have a miserable Christmas and it would be Ian's
fault. "I haven't seen this side of you before, Maggie. I
can't say I like it."

"Me either, but drastic measures are required. Indulge me, okay?" She gave him her most sincere look and dragged a chip through a bowl of onion dip. "You being here makes me happy. Is it so wrong for me to want to be happy? It's been…a long time." Truer words couldn't be spoken.

If he had any sense, he'd go home and forget this day, and especially this night, ever happened. Being here with her and Warny was bittersweet. Wonderful, but it awakened a sense of longing and belonging in him. Made him acutely aware of the strength and acceptance in family, and how much he missed it. He'd forget the sparks that even a simple glance between them ignited. The smell of her hair, the feel of her hugging him, him holding her. The sound of her soft laughter and the serenity in her quiet stillness. He'd forget that when they'd walked the ranch, she'd patted his arm and reached for his hand and paused at the creek to dip her bare toes in the water. It was cold, but she'd had to feel the earth and water of home under her feet. He'd forget all that and her circumstances—if he had sense.

But all of those things bypassed sense and rendered her unforgettable. Every one of them had her knocking not only at the walls of his mind but also at the walls surrounding his heart. He *should* refuse…but this was Maggie. Maggie, who sent him cards on his birthday and at Christmas and Easter. Who not once had forgotten to call on the anniversary of Beth's death to talk him through what would have been merciless, guilt-ridden nights. Maggie, whose notes he'd read so often they were creased and whose conversations he'd played and replayed in his mind to conquer those lonely, hopeless times that plagued him. He couldn't refuse Maggie.

And yet for all those reasons, he shouldn't accept. He wanted her happy but, failing Beth, her murder still unsolved…he had no right to move on with his life. He had enough to regret.

He opened his mouth to inform her that her attempted blackmail had failed, but before he uttered the first sound, the phone rang.

"I've got it." Warny eagerly slid back his chair and snagged the phone from the kitchen counter. "Hello."

He listened for a long moment, his expression sobering, his body tensing. He stuffed a hand into the pocket of his overalls. It was fisted. Ian glanced at Maggie, and one look at her warned him she hadn't missed a thing.

"We'll be all right, Paul," Warny said, then added, "No need. He's sitting at the kitchen table, losing his shirt in a game of Monopoly. I've already asked him. Okay, then. I'll ask him again from you."

Ian homed in. Paul wanted something from him.

"Yes, she's here." Warny glanced at Maggie. "She had a nap on the flight in, but she's got circles the size of black holes under her eyes. Says she's fine, but she likely hadn't slept worth a flip for a week or more, and she's too skinny. Twenty pounds, at least. You do your best, son." Warny hung up the phone and returned to the table.

"What's wrong?" Maggie asked before Ian could. "That was Paul. I know it was."

"It was, and calm down. He and Della are fine. They're just socked in for a couple days. Half the country's immobile due to weather." Warny looked at Ian. "I tried to tell him you'd already agreed to stay put here, but he wasn't in much of a listening mood. He asked if you'd stay on the ranch and help Maggie and me in case Crawford shows up."

Ian had seen the weather report and planned for this in case he was asked. "Suitcase is in the car."

"You knew?"

"In here or out there," Ian said. "I wasn't going to leave you, Maggie. Especially with Paul being away."

She smiled. "Thank you."

He smiled back. "You're welcome."

"You ready to haggle a little over Park Place now?" Warny asked.

The next ten minutes were some of the most intense negotiations Ian had ever witnessed, and they still weren't resolved.

The phone rang. "You two settle this," he said. "I'll get it."

He grabbed the phone from the kitchen counter. "Hello."

"Ian. Ian, can you hear me?"

Madison. His boss and Maggie's lifelong friend. "I hear you." Tons of background noise competed with her voice. "What's up?"

For the next fifteen minutes, she told him, and he grew more and more concerned. By the time the call ended, he had forgotten all about the Monopoly game.

So had Maggie and Warny. He set the phone back into its base and returned to the table. "Madison's stuck, too. She can't get back until a helicopter can airlift her out."

Maggie set the dice on the Monopoly board. "Tell me she's not planning to ruin her Christmas cruise to come back here for me."

"No. She's setting up an emergency conference call. Paul and Della, Mrs. Renault and Jimmy, and you and me, Maggie. Grant's on the ship with her. It's all hands on deck in half an hour."

"Is the boat leaking or what?" Warny asked.

"The ship is fine. Madison is fine. Grant is fine."

"Then what's the emergency?" Maggie set her iced tea down. The table looked bare without a gingerbread house. She'd have to make one.

"We'll know in half an hour."

"We'd best get this game cleared up then." Warny started putting the money back into the slots in the box.

Maggie helped him, pausing to ask Ian, "Does she do this sort of thing often? Emergency conference calls with the entire staff?"

"No. It's rare."

"So just how worried do we need to be about it?"

His eyes sobered. "Madison's never called an emergency meeting without a full-blown crisis attached to it. Typically, a crisis involving someone at the agency."

For her to call one now, when her staff was spread all over the country for Christmas and she was waterlocked on the ocean... "Ominous."

"Knowing Madison—" he dropped the metal car into the box "—we should be very worried."

FOUR

"Yell if you need me." Uncle Warny retreated to his barn apartment.

Jake rested on his bed in the kitchen beside the door. Maggie sat across the kitchen table from Ian. They both had notebooks in front of them and the phone rested in the center of the table, on speakerphone.

When it rang, Ian answered. "We're here, Madison."

"Good. First, welcome home, Maggie. I'm sorry to drag you into this but none of us can get there because of this foul weather and something's come up that can't wait. Frankly, I need your help."

Madison wasn't just serious and bearing bad news, she was scared. Maggie hadn't seen that often, and she hated seeing it now. "You've got it. What's come up?"

"I'll leave it to Ian to fill in the blanks. The upshot is that a few months ago, there was a security breach at the Nest."

Maggie stifled a groan. Only Madison knew discussing the Nest in front of Maggie would be acceptable. If Paul or Ian had to find out, this isn't the way she would have chosen. "Madison, what are you doing?" Paul sounded as shocked as Ian looked.

Confusion riddled Madison's voice. "What?"

No one answered.

"Oh, no." Some light had dawned for Madison. "Maggie, you haven't told him? How could you not tell Paul?"

"What hasn't she told me?" Paul asked.

"Later. I promise." Maggie avoided Ian's eyes. "Go ahead, Madison."

"No." Ian raised his voice. "Not a word, Madison—not about that. You know why, so no excuses. Isn't Maggie in deep enough trouble without adding a security breach to it?"

Maggie frowned at him. "Stop, Ian. Madison isn't doing anything wrong." This was going to go over like a lead balloon. "Does everyone on this call have the necessary clearances to avoid this discussion being a security breach in any way, shape or form?"

Madison didn't hesitate. "Yes."

Maggie had hoped to avoid making Paul aware of her continued active-duty FBI status, but the situation was what it was. Resigned, she began. "What I'm about to say doesn't leave this group. I'm not an outsider—don't ask me to explain, I won't. What I will tell you is that my clearances are current and intact and I know the Nest exists." Ian stared at some distant point on the ceiling. "Paul, you can shoot me later. For now, go ahead, Madison."

Paul's voice elevated. "What do you mean, you're not an outsider?"

"I can't answer you." Maggie laced her hands atop the table. "Think, brother dear. Would Madison breathe a word about the Nest in my presence if I didn't have the necessary clearances?"

"But you can't. You'd have to still be active—" His voice faded into a groan.

Maggie didn't utter a word. Didn't blink or breathe or meet Ian's gaze, though she felt the weight of his on her. At the moment, he wasn't any happier with her than Paul.

"We will discuss this, Margaret Marie Mason."

She winced, betting they would. Paul wouldn't take the news well that she was not only still active with the agency but also still a subject-matter expert to the military. Profiling consultant. Limited exposure, of course, but he'd never known that. "Go on, Madison." With luck, Madison would hurry up and start—

Ian didn't let her. "After Utah, you promised him you'd quit."

"I did," Maggie confessed. "And I intended to keep to it, too. I just got delayed by Crawford."

Madison interceded. "Next time, if you don't want me to out you, give me a little notice that you're breaking your promise."

"I didn't break my promise," Maggie insisted with a sniff. "I just delayed enacting it a little."

Ian rolled his eyes back in his head, mouthed, "Wrong."

She sent him a frosty glare.

"Save it for later. Mrs. Renault will blister her ears for you—or Ian can do it. He's right there and handy." Madison seized control. "Back to the matter at hand. A few months ago there was a security breach at the Nest. Nothing has changed on its status, Maggie. It's still classified and as unmentionable as Area 51, though a few more people have been brought into the need-to-know loop. Access to the facilities is still restricted, and most assigned to the base are not aware the Nest exists in the woods on the base, much less aware of the underground bunkers.

"The Nest has underground bunkers?"

"Yes, Jimmy, it does," Madison told the youngest member on her staff. "But they're not of interest to us at the moment."

Ian seemed surprised by that news, as well. Maggie wasn't, but held her tongue.

"Since the breach, there's been an active investigation to determine who leaked classified information to the press," Madison said. "General Talbot and Colonel Dayton insist that either Paul or someone on staff at Lost, Inc., is responsible."

No one said a word, but the gravity of the situation didn't escape Maggie. Paul would never do that, of course, but then neither would Ian, Madison or Mrs. Renault. Maggie didn't know Jimmy or Madison's new employee, Grant Deaver, well enough to vouch for them.

"When we were active duty—" Madison's voice crackled, the storm wreaking havoc with the phone "—we all were stationed at the base and had access to some part of the Nest. Maggie, we've already established that none of us know the mission there, including Mrs. Renault."

Her husband had been the base commander, before he'd died at his desk, and General Talbot assumed command.

Madison's tone grew more intense. "As for supposed motive, we all have reason to not be enamored with the government."

Taking a sip of iced tea, Maggie absorbed the data, slotted it, falling back into the profiling routine as familiar to her as breathing. Madison had been a POW, left behind and reported dead. Ian had lost Beth. Della's son had been the victim of a man suffering PTSD while she was deployed to Afghanistan. Paul fought for veterans' rights routinely through his organization, Florida Vet Net.

She muted the phone and asked Ian, "What's the short-take on Jimmy?"

"His buddy Bruno took an IED to save him. They didn't have the right gear, but the honchos sent them on a mission headquarters deemed critical anyway. Bruno died. Jimmy didn't."

Anger and survivor's guilt, like Ian. She unmuted the phone. "Madison, why are Talbot and Dayton looking outside the base for the leak? Odds are it's someone—"

"General Talbot is up for a congressional appointment. If he gets it, Colonel Dayton gets command of the Nest. If the leak is one of their own, they can kiss their promotions goodbye."

"Got it." Maggie did, and yet she had a hard time reconciling the kind-eyed man and the colonel who'd helped her escape from Nashville with men who would frame innocents. "Would Talbot do that, Mrs. Renault?" She knew more about everyone than anyone in all of North Bay, including Miss Addie at the café.

"He is his career and has nothing else," Mrs. Renault answered. "If he thought it was over, he might."

Her disappointment was evident. She resented having to consider it a possibility. Understanding that, Maggie asked, "What about Dayton?"

"I don't know."

Translated, that meant, Mrs. Renault had an opinion but wouldn't voice it without evidence to back it up. Not good news. But, to be fair, Talbot and Dayton weren't necessarily out of line. Everyone here did have a bone to pick with the government. Would they pick it? That was the question, and on that the jury was still out. Maggie's instincts said none of them would, but she'd worked too many cases where the unlikely had happened. In battles between ambition and honesty, truth was often the first casualty. Talbot and Dayton would move every mountain to save their jobs and get those promotions. "Okay. So what exactly is the development, Madison?"

"A reporter asked Talbot some point-blank questions."

"Reporters do that. I'm sure if the general didn't want to answer them, he deflect—"

"He's dead, Maggie."

"The reporter is dead?" Her gaze collided with Ian's across the table.

"His body was found a few hours ago on an abandoned dirt road about a quarter mile from the highway on 85. I've emailed everyone a map."

"Bullet to the head, right?" Jimmy asked Madison.

"Car bomb, I'm told, but the forensics are problematic. Apparently, the car was moved to its current location after the explosion."

"Why was it moved?" Maggie asked. "Was that the security breach?" A perimeter breach shouldn't cause this kind of stir, but with a congressional appointment and a command on the line...

"It's significant," Madison said. "Pull up your email. Subject line is Pace."

Ian did on his cell and showed Maggie the screen. It was a photo of a dark-haired man in his early thirties with a wide forehead and a sharp nose.

"That's the reporter, David Pace. He signaled Talbot and Dayton that the breach had occurred."

"How?" Maggie asked.

"By asking them for verification of something at the base."

Surprise streaked through Maggie. "That's the breach?"

Ian stepped in. "Not him asking about the base, Maggie. He specifically asked if the Nest existed, and if it did, for what purpose."

Inside Maggie, alarms blared. "Just like Beth."

Ian shot her a look. "What?"

"That's what Beth was doing at the time she was murdered—investigating something at the base." Surprise joined the alarms. "You didn't know that? How could you not know that?"

"I didn't know it," Ian said. "You know military spouses are told not to bother their soldiers with anything at home they don't absolutely have to bother them with. If they're not focused on the task at hand in a war zone, the results can be catastrophic." Ian stilled and the stunned mumbling ceased. "How did you know it?"

"Beth and I were check-in buddies. We talked several times a day. The last time we spoke, she was agitated. She'd been to see Talbot and Dayton about something she was investigating for the station—"

"What station?" Ian asked.

Maggie lifted a hand. "The TV station where she hoped to work."

Ian sat stunned. "Beth worked at a TV station?"

Beth really didn't bother him with things going on at home. "Well, she was trying to, which is why she was investigating something at the base. Getting the job depended on the outcome of her investigation. Anyway, she was agitated because the meeting hadn't gone well. In fact, Dayton told her to back off and never mention it again."

Ian dragged a hand through his hair. "You'd think she'd have said something…"

Maggie shrugged. "Like you said, spouses are instructed not to bother their soldiers with things going on at home. They can't control them and it causes them to sliver focus. In a nutshell, you were gone and she was trying to do something constructive with her time, Ian. She hadn't yet gotten the job, so there was nothing solid to tell you yet. No big deal."

"It might have been a very big deal. She's dead and now this reporter, David Pace, is, too."

Madison shared the station information with them. "Sorry to dump this all in your laps, but there's nothing the rest of us can do to get there until the weather clears. Detective Cray is my point of contact. Ian, call him with anything you get. He'll call you with anything new on Pace."

"Got it," Ian said, still sounding a little dazed.

Inside, he was reeling. It showed in the tension in his face, the rigid set of his jaw. "We'll keep you posted, Madison."

Maggie ended the call, double-checked to make sure it disconnected. "You okay?" she asked Ian.

"Yeah." He swallowed hard. "In the morning, we'll go talk to this station manager."

"Okay." Maggie frowned. "I'll pull his name off the net."

"Madison will email it, if she hasn't already. She always does a written report." Ian stood up. "It'll say you've been doing military consults, too, won't it?"

Not at all surprised he'd deduced it, she nodded.

"I'm going to head out to the barn now. You get some rest."

She nodded. The evening had been great, but boy had it turned bitter now. He needed some time to himself to process this news about Beth. That he'd missed a stone to turn unnerved him. Likely, he'd be chewing himself up for it the rest of the night.

"Guard her, Jake," Ian told the Rottweiler then moved toward the door, stopped and turned around, then walked back to her.

Standing beside the table, he just stared at her a long minute. It was hard not to speak or flinch, but he needed a minute to reconcile something going on in his head. A war raged in his eyes. "I'm blown away by this news about Beth. I can't believe you knew it all along and didn't tell me."

"I would have told you if I'd known you didn't know it. At first, talking about Beth was too painful, and then you said you'd tracked her movements from when you left until she passed. I had no reason to think you didn't know about the station."

He frowned. "You surprised me with the military consults—I didn't know you did that—but you wouldn't have kept anything about Beth from me. Not intentionally."

"No, I wouldn't have." She let him see the truth in her eyes.

"For the first time in a year, I have a new lead. Thank you, Maggie." He kissed her, clearly intending a quick brush of their lips, but when their mouths touched something happened. Something warm and wonderful and welcome. Something sudden and startling that drew them closer, made them linger, and it felt so…right.

Ian abruptly released her and pulled back. Surprise rippled in his eyes. "I didn't…expect…"

She'd felt it—that grounding, that balance—and she hadn't expected it, either. "I know."

"You, too?"

Her heart raced. She nodded. "Fluke?"

"I don't know." He frowned.

"Should we find out?" She wanted to know. Needed to know.

He curled his arms around her, pulled her close and kissed her again. She didn't think, just reacted, and kissed him back.

When their mouths parted, she felt weak and breathless. She'd wondered what kissing him would be like. Now she knew, and it was better than she'd dreamed. So much better, it couldn't happen again.

He drew back. "Not a fluke." Abject misery lit in his eyes.

Certainly, it reflected in her own. "Definitely not."

He backed away. "Welcome home, Maggie."

"Uh-huh." Too stunned to do more than mumble, she just stood there leaning hard against the back of her chair and watched him walk out the back door.

Now *what* was this electricity between them all about? When had their relationship shifted? How could it shift and neither of them even know it?

The next morning, Ian acted as if nothing happened. Taking her cue from him, Maggie didn't say a word about that kiss or ask a question during breakfast. After they'd eaten, she and Uncle Warny cleaned the kitchen while Ian spoke on the phone with Detective Cray and reviewed the report on Pace.

"Are you ready to get going?" Ian closed a small notebook and tucked it into his shirt pocket. "We have an appointment in an hour. The station manager's name is Brett Lund. That is the same station as Beth's, right?"

Maggie grabbed her purse, checked to make sure her weapon and her new phone were inside. "It is if the station is WKME, yes."

Worry settled on Ian's face. "It is."

Maggie hooked her purse strap on her shoulder. "Are you thinking that these cases are connected?"

"It's a possibility. I'm not sure yet."

"Neither am I. Beth and Pace on the same assignment made it appear so, but why would the manager wait three years to reassign the story? And Beth never specifically mentioned the Nest, just the base. So this could be coincidental."

"It could." Ian took the last sip from his coffee cup. "Hopefully Lund will talk to us."

"He'll be reluctant. He just lost an employee."

"He'll get over it. I lost a wife."

Uncle Warny rubbed at his neck. "If you two want to get there in time for your appointment, you better stop yapping and get moving."

Wordlessly, Maggie and Ian pulled a security check on the Ford Expedition, mindful of Crawford's penchant for car bombs and well aware from Dayton that he could already be in the area. True, there'd been no alerts on the security system, or any calls from the task force warning her, but with Crawford all that meant is one must be even more mindful.

Buckled into her seat, Maggie waited for Ian to say something about kissing her. But he didn't speak a word about that or anything else, and frankly she didn't know what to think about it. She kept waiting, but to no avail. About five miles from the station, she couldn't take the silence anymore. "Did you gain any new information from Detective Cray?"

"Yes, I did. Sorry. I should have told you. I'm just a little preoccupied." He looked genuinely contrite. "The coroner hasn't issued a formal report yet, but from visuals, he says Pace's death wasn't due to the car bomb."

"What was the cause of death?"

"Uncertain, pending the outcome of his examination."

Maggie frowned. The man was hedging. "What does he think was the cause of death?"

"Apparent suicide." Ian looked skeptical.

"You obviously don't agree. Any particular reason?"

"A couple of them." Ian spared her a glance. "But the main one is that when they found Pace—inside a car gutted by an explosion—he wasn't burned and he had on an unusual pair of shoes."

"So he was placed in the car after it exploded?"

"Had to be postdetonation."

Why would someone do that? "What was unusual about his shoes?"

"They were neon blue."

"Okay. And that's significant because…"

"Della's stalker wore neon blue shoes."

"A lot of guys do." Hadn't she just seen a pair in Dayton's bag on the plane?

"You don't understand. The neon blue shoes helped nail Jeff Jackson as Della's stalker."

"Ian, I'm sure any physical object's been used in a crime somewhere by someone."

"Detective Cray says Jeff denies involvement in many of the attacks on Della and Paul, but the neon blue shoes were found in his hotel room. Blue shoes were spotted by witnesses in several of the bombings and in the fire that burned down Della's cottage." He twisted his lips. "I know what you're thinking."

"What?"

"That jails are full of people claiming to be innocent."

She had been. "They are, Ian."

"We know some things Jeff did do. But this with the shoes isn't sitting right." Ian's gaze shifted to the rearview mirror. "Maybe Jeff isn't Mr. Blue Shoes."

"Mr. Blue Shoes?"

"The guy who pulled the bombing attacks on Della and Paul."

That was a leap she couldn't make. "Cray caught Jackson with hard evidence—"

"That was the shoes. They could have been planted."

"There's no evidence of that, and Jeff Jackson did pull the stunt with the ambulance that nearly killed Paul and Della."

"True. But there's also no evidence—none, Maggie—that Jeff knew anything about explosives, yet bombs were used against Paul and Della multiple times." He draped an arm over the steering wheel. "I'm telling you, something feels...off."

"Okay." She trusted his instincts. They had proved sound. "We'll keep that in mind. When Pace's body was found, he had on blue shoes." It could be something or nothing. They needed more information to know. "It isn't like they're rare."

"Men's blue aquatic shoes?"

She nodded. "Even Dayton has a pair." Catching Ian's odd look, she explained. "I saw them in his bag at the airport, when he was transferring my weapon."

"When we're done here, maybe we can go talk to Jeff Jackson, and get Grant Deaver busy pinpointing where Talbot and Dayton were at the time of Pace's death."

"Good idea—not that either will be directly involved, but maybe we can connect someone to them who could be."

"My guess is they were in Nashville—with you."

"Wouldn't that be an airtight alibi?"

"Yeah, I guess it would." Ian pulled into a parking slot in front of WKME and cut the engine. "One other thing you need to know before we go in there."

"What?"

"Cray believes David Pace was inside the Nest's perimeter fence—soil samples taken from residual evidence on his clothes."

Surely he wouldn't be killed for that. Jailed or fined, maybe, but murdered? Not likely...except for Beth. Maybe Pace had refused to back off asking questions about the Nest. "I'll make a note of that, too."

Ian looked at her as if he wanted to say something more but couldn't quite make himself do it. She smoothed her black slacks, tugged at the sleeves of her red sweater, unsure if she wanted to push for questions or answers she might not like. But if she couldn't talk to him freely...well, there was no one left. "What?"

"I owe you an apology, Maggie."

"For what?"

"I should never have kissed you. I'm not sure why I did—the second time, I mean."

The urge to cry hit her hard and fast. Not expecting it, she had a hard time burying the swell of emotion that rose with it. She couldn't show it, of course. If he regretted kissing her and she did show it, she could wreck their relationship. Burying her own feelings on the matter, she asked, "What kiss?"

He frowned. "Now you owe me an apology."

She smiled. "You can't have it both ways."

"Were you really unaffected, because it sure seemed like you were kissing me back."

"I was?" That got to him. And it should. She'd been affection-starved for nearly four years. Of course she was affected. That didn't mean she was crazy enough to do it again, especially not with a man who apologized for kissing her, and even more important, not with Crawford on her heels. Ian could end up dead.

"You were, and you know it."

Maggie opened the door and stepped outside. If she stayed in the SUV, she'd have to admit the truth or lie, and though this little discussion left her ego pretty battered, she couldn't make herself lie.

Ian slammed his door and pressed the remote lock until the horn beeped. "I can't believe you won't just admit you liked it."

She slid him a sideward look meant to melt steel. He apologized and then wanted her to admit she liked it? Not in this lifetime. "Maybe I didn't." She started across the lot, heading for the sidewalk.

He caught up near the station's glass front door. "Of course you did."

"If I did—and I'm not saying I did, mind you—I wouldn't read much into it, Ian. I've been alone a long time. It doesn't take much to get my attention." That should shake his cocky attitude. "But keeping my attention is a whole different matter." *Thank you, Madison McKay.* If not for remembering that about her, the thought wouldn't have occurred to Maggie.

He gave her a slow smile that snatched her breath. Before her eyes, it melted under a heap of worry. "You liked it."

Seeing that the possibility troubled him, she hiked her chin. "It was nothing. Like I said, what kiss?" She nodded. "Now hush and get the door."

They cleared security and an escort led them into a corner office on the second floor. A woman with blue contact lenses—no one had eyes that blue—came out from behind her desk and ushered them into the inner sanctum where Brett Lund sat behind a very large oak desk littered with enough files to fill a two-drawer cabinet.

In his mid-forties, Lund was graying at the temples and nearly bald on the crown. His rumpled gray suit told the tale that he'd been at the office all night, likely staying close awaiting informational updates on David Pace to come in or cross the wire.

"Good morning." Lund stood up and extended his hand, introduced himself and then seated them in his gray leather visitors' chairs. Returning to his own seat, he rocked back. "I accepted this meeting, but I have no idea why you want to talk to me. Is this a professional visit, Dr. Crane, or a personal one?"

"What's the difference?"

The starch in Lund's voice doubled. "Frankly, if you're here on behalf of Lost, Inc., I have nothing to say to you. If it's personal, I might."

"Then let's make it a personal visit." Ian clasped the arm of his chair.

"I'm assuming you're here about David Pace. If so, and you read the paper or heard the news, then you know what I know."

"We're not here about David Pace." Ian's gaze narrowed. "We're here about my wife, Beth."

The starch wilted. Lund tried to reclaim it. "If this is about your wife, then why—" he swiveled his gaze to Maggie "—are you here?"

Already, he was in cease-and-desist-and-admit-nothing mode. "Mr. Lund, these are serious matters. Lives have been lost. Let's not diminish the seriousness of that by playing childish games," Maggie said, already weary of his evasion tactics. First, they were elementary, and second, he was lousy at implementing them. Time to throw a few flames and see if he fanned them. "I know for a fact Beth Crane was working for you. I know that you hired her as an investigative reporter—"

"On a trial basis."

"On a trial basis," Maggie conceded, "and I know she was working on an assignment—"

"I hadn't yet given her any assignments."

Defensive. He knew far more than he wanted to share. Creating distance, self-preservation instincts kicking in. Oh, yes. He wanted to disassociate. But that was not going to happen. "Beth was neck-deep in a personal investigation. She brought her findings to you, and based on those findings, you agreed to hire her pending the outcome of her investigation." Maggie frowned at him. "You asked why I'm here. Simply put, the reason is because I know the truth. Attempting to placate me with half-truths and/or omissions won't work." She dipped her chin and studied his eyes. "Under the circumstances, I'd think you'd have better judgment than to opt for trying them."

He stopped rocking. Stilled. "What circumstances?"

Maggie played a hunch. "First Beth and now David Pace, and you ask me what circumstances?" She grunted. "Mr. Lund, surely not. To do that would make you either incompetent or deliberately deceptive. I don't believe for a second that a man achieves your position being either. Now, let's be logical and efficient. You can talk with us or with Detective Cray. Your call."

Lund had the grace to flush and sank back in his seat. No starch left, he now sat limp.

Ian's glance at her revealed an admiration of her skills. He shifted focus to Lund. "What exactly was Beth investigating?"

Lund darted a look at the office door, as if for reassurance that it was closed and what he revealed would remain private. "The Nest."

Ian stiffened and so did Maggie. There's no way Beth or Lund should even know the Nest existed, and no way Maggie or Ian could admit knowing about it or even ask him for information about it. "And what was Pace investigating?"

Lund aged ten years before her eyes. "The Nest."

Ian's grip on the chair arm had his knuckles white. "Was Pace's death suicide?"

A long moment passed with Lund chewing his lower lip. "That's what I'm being told, but it's just preliminary findings. Final's not confirmed yet."

"Do you believe the preliminary findings are true?"

Lund's jaw locked. He glanced away, paused and then swiveled his gaze back to Ian. "I have a wife and two kids, Dr. Crane." His eyes clouded, turned deadpan flat. "The truth is whatever the authorities tell me is the truth."

Two reporters dead…Maggie understood Lund's position. Beneath the veneer lay turmoil. Turmoil and raw fear. "Why did you wait three years to assign Pace to the investigation?"

"The file was misplaced." Lund shrugged. "It just resurfaced."

Rage simmered in Ian. Maggie felt it radiate from him like a furnace blast.

"Stop. My wife is dead and you dare to sit there and lie to me. You owe me more. You owe her more." He paused and leashed his tone. "You knew drug-seeking thugs didn't invade our home and kill her. You knew it was this investigation, and you were afraid you'd be next."

Maggie agreed with Ian, watched closely for Lund's reaction, taking special note of his body language. It rarely lied.

He stiffened, pursed his lips, blinked hard and fast. "I've given you two leeway out of respect for your wife, Dr. Crane." Lund stood up. "But now this meeting is over."

Ian stood and reached over the desk for Lund, clasped him by the shirtfront. "Tell me the truth!"

Lund sputtered and stretched, pressed a button on the lip of his desk, no doubt summoning security.

"Ian, no." Maggie wedged between the desk and Ian. "Let him go." She looked up at him, saw the moment what he was doing registered in his eyes. "Ian, let him go."

He opened his hand, spread his fingers wide and then stepped back. "You knew or suspected Beth was murdered for this investigation and you still sent in Pace. He has a wife and kids, too. Did you think about that? Did Pace know about Beth, or did you send him in blind?"

"I have no idea who or what Pace did or did not know. Now get out of my office."

"With pleasure," Ian said. "Expect a visit from Detective Cray. You can explain yourself to him. Don't look so worried just yet. Not reporting what you know about Beth's death and admitting you sent David Pace into harm's way blinder than a bat will be easy. It's the other explanations you'll have to give that you need to worry about."

"You threatening me?"

"Don't be absurd."

"What other explanations?" Lund shot Ian a haughty look. "To whom?"

"To David Pace's family…and to your own." Ian

leaned over the desk. "Everyone in North Bay and beyond is going to know what you did, Lund—and what
you didn't do. I wonder how your wife and kids are
going to feel about you then."

He paled and glared past Ian's shoulder to the security guard entering the office. "Get them out of here—
and don't let them back in."

The guard looked confused, focused on Ian. "Hi,
Doc."

"Jesse." He nodded. "How's MaryAnne?"

"Fine. In the grocery store when we ran into you and
her back was hurting—you were right. Her doc checked
her out and it was a kidney stone. She's fine now."

"I'm glad." Ian spared Lund a hard look filled with
disdain.

"Get out!" Lund bellowed. "All of you get out of
my office!"

Jesse reacted first. "I'll walk you out, Doc."

"Thanks." Ian headed toward the door. "You remember Maggie Mason, don't you?"

"Paul's sister. I sure do." He smiled at her. "Good to
have you home, Miss Maggie."

"Thank you." She was glad to be home, but in all the
hours she'd dreamed of her homecoming, it had been
nothing like this.

Jesse opened the station's front door. "Sorry Mr.
Lund treated you like he did."

"He's under a lot of stress."

"Yes, sir. He's been terrorizing the whole station
since he heard about Mr. Pace." Jesse's face turned
ruddy. "I'm afraid I can't let you back in, but if you
need anything, call me. I'll help you if I can."

"Thank you, Jesse."

Maggie and Ian stepped outside and she paused on

the sidewalk to study him. *Rattled, devastated* and *outraged* all came to mind. She held out her hand. "Best let me drive."

He didn't argue, just passed her the keys and got in on the passenger's side of the Expedition then slammed the door with a lot more force than was necessary.

"Time for extreme action," Maggie mumbled to herself on her walk to the driver's side of the SUV. *Lord, I could use a little help here.*

She got in and cranked the engine, looked over and saw a billboard for Shady Pines cemetery.

Of course.

Ian called Detective Cray, filled him in on what they'd learned from Lund, requested a meeting at the jail with Jeff Jackson, learned Jackson hadn't yet been transferred to the state correctional facility so Ian could drop in anytime, and warned Cray that Lund wouldn't be cooperative about sharing anything he knew for fear of his life and the lives of his family members.

A part of Ian understood that fear and respected it. After Beth, how could he not? But inside, he was furious. Two years, he'd searched for answers full-time, and he'd continued searching for her killer since he'd hired on at Lost, Inc. He understood now that drugs hadn't been involved but he had a hard time wrapping his mind around the fact that Lund knew or at least suspected Beth's murder had been tied to her investigation and he'd remained silent.

All this time wasted on wild-goose chases. What kind of investigator was he, anyway? Maggie had been back less than twenty-four hours and already she'd made more progress than he had in three years. And the way she'd handled Lund…impressive.

"You okay?" Maggie asked.

Lost in his own thoughts, Ian forced himself to shift his attention to her. "Not really."

She nodded and cut the engine. "Come with me."

Only then did he realize she'd stopped—and where she'd stopped. "Why are we at Shady Pines?"

"Beth is buried here." Maggie left the SUV and waited for him outside.

Ian got out and closed the door. "I know where she's buried, Maggie. I put her in the ground. What I want to know is why we're at the cemetery right now."

She tilted her head. "I couldn't come to her funeral. I knew about the station but didn't realize there could be a connection between it and her death. I had no reason to believe anything other than what the police concluded about a drug addict breaking into a doctor's home seeking drugs. No one did…except Lund. Maggie twisted the car keys in her hand. "I did know the colonel told her to back off but many things go on at a military installation. I didn't know she knew about the Nest. Anyway, I need to tell Beth I'm sorry."

That took the wind out of his sails. "You have nothing to apologize for. I failed her. Not you."

Maggie's eyes looked haunted. "She was my friend." She swept the air with a fingertip. "Which way?"

He nodded right. "Second row, third grave."

"Come with me." Maggie's eyes were dry, but her voice sounded thin and reedy.

His wouldn't, so he kept quiet. Inside, he felt like a jumbled mass of snapping livewires and crackling electrical shocks.

Maggie stood before Beth's grave, gently stroked the headstone, the embedded copper angel so like the medallion Beth had worn all the time. Long minutes passed where Maggie apparently was having a silent conversation with Beth inside her mind or she was praying. He didn't know which.

Finally, she bent down and touched the petal of the fresh yellow carnations in a vase on the grave. "It's lovely that you still send her flowers, Ian." Maggie looked at him and smiled through a face drawn and tense. "Do you need a few minutes alone?"

"No, she's heard it all."

"Why are you angry?" Maggie looked up at him.

"Lund knew."

"He suspected something, yes. But he didn't know, and he didn't want to be buried next to Beth, or worse, he didn't want to see his wife and kids buried next to Beth."

"After Pace, he had to know. But he said nothing to Cray."

"He doesn't want to die." She turned to face Ian. "I've been in that position. I understand his fear."

"You would have told me."

"I think I would have, but I don't know. I didn't tell Paul how close Crawford had come to killing me."

"That's different, Maggie. You were protecting Paul."

"Maybe. But I was terrified if I said anything, I'd make him a target again. So I didn't. Maybe it's that way for Lund, too. That's all I'm saying."

"Do you think he knows who's behind the killings?"

He believed Pace had been murdered. So did she. "No, I think he doesn't know, which is why he's even more afraid. If he knew, he'd report the person to diminish the threat. He doesn't know."

Anger roiled inside Ian. "You think Dayton and General Talbot are involved?"

"Maybe. Honestly, doubtful. It's too obvious. They'd be more subtle."

"I agree." Frustration flooded him.

"But it's too soon to tell." Maggie placed a hand on his sleeve. "Ian, you need to let go of the anger."

"Impossible."

"Essential." Maggie stroked his sleeve. "It clouds your mind, erodes your peace. Beth is dead, Ian. She doesn't want or need your anger."

"How do you know what Beth wants or needs?"

Maggie covered his lips with her fingertips. "Because if I were murdered, I'd want those I left behind to live and love and laugh. I'd want them to be happy and enjoy their lives. To know they were so filled with rage they were—"

"Stuck?"

She nodded. "It would break my heart."

"I don't know how to stop," he whispered. "Anger is all I have left."

"No, it's not." Maggie stepped closer. "You have me." She wrapped her arms around his waist and rested her head against his chest. His heart thudded against her ear.

Warmth. Comfort. He closed his arms around Maggie, let holding her fill his senses. The anger in him weakened, countered by compassion and caring. It didn't dissipate, just faded, there but not as potent or all-consuming. Once again with Maggie, he was the lucky one.

He turned his head. Glimpsed something behind the headstone. What was it? Stepping around, he saw the object propped against the slick marble and stiffened. "Maggie, get to the SUV. Do it now."

"What?" She reached into her purse automatically and withdrew her gun.

Ian quickly scanned the cemetery but saw no one else. Saw nothing out of place. "Take cover."

"From what?"

He grabbed her by the arm and rushed back to the SUV. "Go, go, go!"

She fumbled but keyed the ignition, threw the gearshift into Reverse and hit the gas.

Gravel spewed, the tires spun and grabbed, and she braked hard, then switched to Drive and stomped the gas pedal. "What are we running from?"

Finally, Ian spotted him. Little more than a speck hunched down behind a tomb, he wore all black—except for his neon blue shoes.

A bullet whizzed past the SUV and sent bark flying off an oak lining the road. The sound roared through the cemetery, echoing off the graves.

Maggie fishtailed through the gravel to the main road and hit the pavement going sixty.

"Who was that?"

"I suspect it was the real Mr. Blue Shoes." Ian dialed his phone, reported the incident to Cray, finishing with, "We're getting Maggie back to the ranch. We'll email you statements." He then hung up.

Maggie frowned. "I saw the shoes, too."

"What about in Illinois?" Ian asked. "You said you watched him make his way across the yard. Did he have on blue shoes, then?"

She tried to remember but couldn't. "I don't know. I was so focused on the gun in his hand, I didn't look at his feet. The gun and the mask and that he was in all black. That's all I recall."

Ian unzipped his jacket and the sound brought a flash of a memory to her mind. One of Dayton moving her weapon bag to bag on the airplane. Slowing to the limit, she headed toward the police station. "Ian, yesterday on the plane, Colonel Dayton switched my gun from my bag to his."

"I remember. He returned your weapon once we cleared the terminal."

Maggie nodded. "But that's not what's significant."

"What is?"

"When he put my gun in his bag, I saw a pair of neon blue shoes."

He processed that. A link between Mr. Blue Shoes and Talbot and Dayton, or a coincidence? "You're sure it was Dayton's bag?"

"Yes. Well, no. Not really." She pulled alongside a green truck at the stoplight. "General Talbot actually carried it. But he handed it back to Dayton after he'd cleared security." Uncertainty flooded her. "It could have belonged to either of them."

"So Mr. Blue Shoes could still be either of them—or Crawford, or someone else entirely."

"Crawford?"

"He's good with bombs."

They worked through the time line and on the dates Blue Shoes had been active here, Crawford hadn't been active during those same times against Maggie. "Surely the man hasn't decided to take on all of North Bay to get back at me."

"Maybe it isn't just about you anymore," Ian said. "Paul survived, too. You said he hates loose ends, and you and Paul survived him." Ian frowned. "Where are you going?"

"To the police station. I want to talk to Cray about all this."

Ian motioned her to take a left at the corner. "They closed the old pass-through by the theater." It was shaped like a castle. "You have to go around it now. It's a kids' park."

Maybe Crawford was Blue Shoes. Maybe he was taking revenge on North Bay that she and Paul hadn't died. "Why are you not telling me everything, Ian?"

He turned and looked at her. "What?"

"You didn't see the man wearing blue shoes until later. What did you see first—when you told me to get to the SUV?"

"Park over there." He pointed to an empty slot.

When she had, she turned off the engine and removed the key. "I'm not moving until you tell me."

Regret filled his eyes. "You're right. I'd hoped you hadn't noticed and I could wait to tell you after we were back at the ranch. But, as usual, you're too smart for your own good."

"Smart enough to know you're stalling."

He clasped her hand, covered it with both of his. "There was something propped against the backside of Beth's headstone, Maggie."

"What?"

"A black rose."

FIVE

Detective Cray walked out of the police station with a package tucked under his arm. "Ian." He nodded, and then smiled at Maggie. "Maggie Mason, it's good to have you home."

"Thank you." She smiled back. After the warmth of the SUV, the air felt cool and she wrapped her jacket tighter around her.

"I am worried that your arrival wasn't a little more… quiet." He dipped his chin. "Madison called and gave me a heads-up that you were here in case Crawford showed up. So did Della, who didn't know that Paul had already called."

They were worried. With good cause. So was she. "Crawford could be here already."

Cray held up a finger, walked away from the building toward a little greenbelt area filled with benches, motioning for them to join him. "Safer to talk out here. The walls in there have ears."

Maggie had run into the same situation too often to ask questions. Some liked being a contact point for the media. It made them feel important. And no matter how careful others tried to be, there were always leaks. She studied Cray. He had aged well. Late forties, graying ever so slightly, in decent shape, and he lacked the hard edge most in his line of work acquired as a self-defense mechanism. When you deal with the dark side of people all the time and wade through the trenches with them and their victims, it's tough not to get hard. She admired him for fighting it.

Ian stood back to the brick building and scanned the lot, clearly still uneasy because of the shot fired at the cemetery. "What is it that you don't want overheard?"

"Pace was murdered. That's not yet official, but if the coroner comes back with anything else I'll be shocked."

No surprise there. "You have officers at the cemetery now, right?" Maggie asked. When he nodded, she went on. "You need to call them and let them know to photograph the backside of Beth Crane's headstone."

"Why?" he asked, perplexed.

"There's a black rose propped on it."

"Crawford." Cray's brows furrowed and his breath escaped, fogging the cold air.

Maggie glanced from Ian to Cray, waited for two uniformed officers to exit the building and walk past them. "This hasn't been made public, but Crawford has left me a black rose twice before. He also left one for his second victim."

"I thought it was a dozen."

He'd been briefed. "That's only after he kills them. The single rose is before." Was it intended for Ian or her? Had to be Ian. She hadn't planned on going there until she'd seen the cemetery sign.

His concern etched lines deeper in his face, dragged at the corners of his mouth. "This isn't good news."

It wasn't. But he hadn't yet heard the worst of it. She shot Ian a questioning look.

Cray missed it and asked, "Did you see the shooter out there?"

"From a distance," Ian answered, stuffing his hands into the pockets of his jacket. The tip of his nose was pink and the stiff breeze had his eyes watering. "Enough to know he was dressed in solid black, wearing a mask and he had on neon blue shoes."

Cray's eyes widened then disappointment filled them. "I was afraid of that. I'm so sorry." Cray let his gaze wander, shifted the package from one arm to tuck it under the other. "After you called, I pulled the blue shoes from the evidence room and went to see Jeff Jackson. Prison's overcrowded so we're stuck with him until they free up some space."

"We hoped to talk to him, too."

"Not necessary, Ian." Cray frowned. "He's been calling Della every day, swearing he had nothing to do with the bombings and that the shoes weren't his. Frankly, we didn't pay a lot of attention to him. We found them in his hotel room, so why would we?"

"But you are now," Ian said. "What happened?"

"I took the shoes to his jail cell and asked him to try them on." Cray's expression turned grim. "He was relieved to do it."

"They didn't fit." Maggie stifled a gasp.

"No, they didn't."

Ian looked at Maggie. "Crawford could be Mr. Blue Shoes." He frowned. "Do you know where he was during the time Della and Paul were under attack?"

"If I did, he'd be under arrest."

"No incidents during that time?"

"I ran the dates, remember? No activity with me until two days after Paul said the situation here was resolved. Well, when he thought it was resolved for the first time.

There was a time gap, and then Ian told me Jackson had been arrested. I was in Illinois then."

"Where were you the first time—when Paul thought the situation was resolved but it wasn't?" Ian asked.

"Fleeing Montana." She'd had to leave in a hurry then, too. Abandoned all her gorgeous big sky landscapes. She swallowed a sigh.

"That's what prompted your move to Illinois? An incident that happened after Paul and Della's problem was believed resolved but wasn't?"

She nodded. "I came home from the grocery store and found a black rose attached to a canvas on my easel with a pushpin. I grabbed my paintbrushes and left."

Cray listened with obvious interest. "Are you telling me that there have been no sightings or activity on Crawford during the time that Blue Shoes was active here?"

"I'd want to double-check the dates before officially verifying, but we ran them once already and found nothing. So I don't believe so. If one was active, the other wasn't."

Awareness gleamed in Cray's eyes. "You let him chase you so he won't kill others." Worry of the worse kind settled in. "Maggie, he's a mastermind killer—"

"Yes, he is, and actually, just him chasing me isn't accurate, though it happens." She sniffed against the cold settling in on her. "I'm always trying to find him, too." The shot at the cemetery fired again through her mind. "Though once again it seems he's found me first."

"Or someone wants you to think he has," Ian countered, rubbing his jaw. "Either way, we need to get you back to the ranch, where security is tight."

"He had no way of knowing I would be at that cemetery this afternoon."

"He could have suspected it," Ian said, then shrugged. "We stopped and bought flowers. If we were spotted…"

"True." That sat easier on her shoulders than Crawford targeting Ian.

"Either way, you two watch yourselves."

Ian nodded at the detective. "We'll post you on anything we find out."

"About Lund." Cray seemed more than reluctant to say what he must. "I'm sorry, Ian, but we won't be finding out anything from him."

Ian grunted his disgust. "He's lawyered up."

"No, it isn't that."

"Then what is it? Is he refusing to talk?" Maggie knew how to tackle that problem. Reluctant didn't mean impossible, just hostile.

"He can't talk." Cray grimaced. "The call came in while you two were on the way over here." He hardened his voice. "According to Jesse, the station security guard—"

"We know Jesse," Ian said.

Cray nodded. "Not long after you left his office, Lund took a phone call. His door was closed and neither Jesse nor Lund's secretary know who he called or what was said, but both of them heard Lund's muffled, heated voice. It wasn't a pleasant call. We're looking into the phone records now to find out who was on the other end."

"Why not just ask Lund?" Ian asked.

"Can't." Cray swallowed hard, bobbing his Adam's apple. "Word from the feds—they're primary on this because of the Pace incident, our guys weren't even allowed on scene—is when Lund got off the phone, he put a bullet in his mouth."

Ian squeezed his eyes shut.

Maggie shook. Hard. "I'll keep him and his family in my prayers."

"Can you drive?" Maggie asked Ian.

"Sure."

Still shaken about Lund, she passed the keys. "We need to stop at the grocery store."

"Okay." Gauging by the set of his jaw, Ian wasn't crazy about the idea. "I'm assuming it's important?"

Fishing her phone from her purse, she dialed and answered him simultaneously. "Very. I need all the stuff to make a gingerbread house." He looked at her as if she'd lost her mind, and she frowned to let him know that she hadn't missed it. "It's five days until Christmas. It's a tradition."

"I know, we spent hours on the phone while you were making the last couple. But I'm not sure it's a good idea to linger anywhere away from the ranch until we find out who put that rose on Beth's grave or took a shot at us, Maggie."

She held up a wait-a-minute finger. "This is Sparrow," she said into the phone. "It's possible Gary Crawford is in North Bay, Florida. Could be a copycat— probably is—I can't be sure at this point. I'll email details to the task force within the hour. Right now, I need satellite imagery." She tilted the phone and lowered her voice. "Ian, get me the coordinates for where they found David Pace's car."

He nodded, and she went on. "A reporter here purportedly committed suicide, but his car was bombed. He wasn't burned and he had on neon blue shoes that are significant to another case. His boss, the station manager, put a bullet in his mouth just after questioning.

And a few hours ago, a man took a potshot at me at a cemetery. He left a black rose on a headstone significant to our case, and he had on neon blue shoes, which is significant to the other case." Maggie paused but didn't hear anything coming from the other end. There was nothing uncommon about that. "I want imagery of these coordinates—" She took them from Ian, relayed them, then added, "Extend out ten miles in all directions. I believe the car was moved after the explosion—no residual evidence of it exploding at the scene—and I'm positive the victim wasn't in the car when it exploded. He wasn't burned." She again paused. "ETA?" she asked, seeking an idea of the estimated time of arrival of the images.

A pause, then the speaker, who could have been man or woman, said, "Five hours, thirty-two minutes."

"Thank you." Maggie hung up and stowed her phone.

"It takes us weeks to get satellite images." Ian grunted. "I'm impressed."

"Don't be. We're not that efficient. I went commercial."

"So do we. It still takes weeks."

"One of the few perks of playing cat-and-mouse with a serial killer. When you say you need something, people assume you need it right now to survive. Unfortunately, you usually do."

Ian held his silence though his expression darkened. He parked in the Publix parking lot and they went inside. Maggie grabbed a cart and began stuffing items into it. "Do you like cornbread or bread stuffing?"

"Either. But herb-seasoned is my favorite."

"With sausage and apples?"

He nodded.

She smiled. "Me, too."

"How do you switch gears like this?" Ian pushed the cart while she dumped items into the basket. She attacked the supermarket like a telemarketer on speed dial. "You don't seem rattled. How can you not be rat— you don't think it's Crawford. You seriously think a copycat shot at us."

"I think it's highly likely." She grabbed a box of graham crackers, debated, then snatched a second one and dropped them in the buggy. "But honestly, when you're running all the time, you get used to acting anyway. You don't wait until later on anything because you never know what later is going to bring. To have any kind of life, you have to snatch what you can when you can." She shrugged and dropped two boxes of powdered sugar into the basket. "For me, this is normal."

"I'm so sorry." He followed her and they checked out. When he'd loaded the groceries and gotten into the SUV, he muttered, "I knew running was rough on you. I knew at times you got close to him and he got close to you, but I guess I didn't have a real understanding of what that meant in actual life terms and what it's been like for you until today."

"I'm glad you've been spared." She smiled. "Hey, let's get dinner at Miss Addie's Café and bring it home. Uncle Warny loves her lemon meringue pie."

"Call and tell her what you want." He passed her his phone. "She's number two on speed dial."

Maggie grinned. "Who's number one?"

"You."

Her heart lurched. It shouldn't be reacting with a thrill that she rated important to him—he was sorry he'd kissed her—but that seemed to matter only to her logic. Her concerns about Crawford didn't weigh in with sense, either. Or his concerns about Beth. "Ian, do you

Get **2** Books **FREE!**

Love Inspired® Books,
a leading publisher of inspirational romance fiction, presents

Love Inspired. **SUSPENSE**
RIVETING INSPIRATIONAL ROMANCE

A series of edge-of-your-seat suspense novels that reinforce important lessons about life, faith and love!

FREE BOOKS!
Get two free books by acclaimed, inspirational authors!

FREE GIFTS!
Get two exciting surprise gifts absolutely free!

2 FREE BOOKS

Love Inspired. **SUSPENSE**
RIVETING INSPIRATIONAL ROMANCE

▲ To get your 2 free books and 2 free gifts, affix this peel-off sticker to the reply card and mail it today!

We'd like to send you two free books to introduce you to the Love Inspired® Suspense series. Your two books have a combined cover price of $11.50 or more in the U.S. and $13.50 or more in Canada, but they are yours free! We'll even send you two wonderful surprise gifts. You can't lose!

Each of your **FREE** books is filled with riveting inspiration suspense featuring Christian character facing challenge to their faith.... and their lives!

FREE BONUS GIFTS!

We'll send you two wonderful surprise gifts, worth about $10, absolutely FREE, just for giving Love Inspired Suspense books a try! Don't miss out— MAIL THE REPLY CARD TODAY!

Visit us at www.ReaderService.

GET 2 FREE BOOKS!

HURRY!
Return this card today to get 2 FREE Books and 2 FREE Bonus Gifts!

Love Inspired
SUSPENSE
RIVETING INSPIRATIONAL ROMANCE

YES! Please send me the 2 FREE Love Inspired® Suspense books and 2 free gifts for which I qualify. I understand that I am under no obligation to purchase anything further, as explained on the back of this card.

affix
free
books
sticker
here

❏ I prefer the regular-print edition
123/323 IDL FNST

❏ I prefer the larger-print edition
110/310 IDL FNST

Please Print

FIRST NAME

LAST NAME

ADDRESS

APT.#   CITY

STATE/PROV.   ZIP/POSTAL CODE

Offer limited to one per household and not applicable to series that subscriber is currently receiving.
Your Privacy – The Reader Service is committed to protecting your privacy. Our Privacy Policy is available online at www.ReaderService.com or upon request from the Reader Service. We make a portion of our mailing list available to reputable third parties that offer products we believe may interest you. If you prefer that we not exchange your name with third parties, or if you wish to clarify or modify your communication preferences, please visit us at www.ReaderService.com/consumerschoice or write to us at Reader Service Preference Service, P.O. Box 9062, Buffalo, NY 14269. Include your complete name and address.

▼ DETACH AND MAIL CARD TODAY! ▼

© 2012 HARLEQUIN ENTERPRISES LIMITED

Printed in the U.S.A

LIS-LA-12C

The Reader Service – Here's How it Works:

Accepting your 2 free books and 2 free mystery gifts (gifts valued at approximately $10.00) places you under no obligation to buy anything. You may keep the books and gifts and return the shipping statement marked "cancel." If you do not cancel, about a month later we will send you 4 additional books and bill you just $4.49 each for the regular-print edition or $4.99 each for the larger-print edition in the U.S. or $4.99 each for the regular-print edition or $5.49 each for the larger-print edition in Canada. That's a savings of at least 22% off the cover price. It's quite a bargain! Shipping and handling is just 50¢ per book in the U.S. and 75¢ per book in Canada.* You may cancel at any time, but if you choose to continue, every month we'll send you 4 more books, which you may either purchase at the discount price or return to us and cancel your subscription. *Terms and prices subject to change without notice. Prices do not include applicable taxes. Sales tax applicable in N.Y. Canadian residents will be charged applicable taxes. Offer not valid in Quebec. All orders subject to credit approval. Books received may not be as shown. Credit or debit balances in a customer's account(s) may be offset by any other outstanding balance owed by or to the customer. Please allow 4 to 6 weeks for delivery. Offer available while quantities last.

▲ If offer card is missing write to: The Reader Service, P.O. Box 1867, Buffalo, NY 14240-1867 or visit www.ReaderService.com ▲

BUSINESS REPLY MAIL
FIRST-CLASS MAIL   PERMIT NO. 717   BUFFALO, NY

POSTAGE WILL BE PAID BY ADDRESSEE

THE READER SERVICE
PO BOX 1867
BUFFALO NY 14240-9952

NO POSTAGE
NECESSARY
IF MAILED
IN THE
UNITED STATES

think maybe one day…" She couldn't make this man-and-woman personal. She almost did, but she couldn't. It just wasn't fair.

"One day, what?"

"Nothing." She wrinkled her nose at him. "I was being silly, dreaming things I have no right to dream."

"I know what you mean," he confessed. "I do it, too."

She studied him, but even her training didn't help decipher that remark. "It's a shame we can't run down to the courthouse and get a license for it, isn't it?"

"A license to dream?" he asked.

"Yeah. Wouldn't that be something? Bet they'd issue a million of them a week. Hey—" she pointed "—you're passing up Miss Addie's."

He hit the brakes. "Sorry." As soon as he parked, he rushed inside and came back out carrying three paper bags full of food. He stowed them in the back and then got in. The hint of a smile curved his lips. "You must be hungry."

"Starved." She laughed. "I love Miss Addie's cooking. I wanted everything, so actually I restrained myself."

He laughed out loud. "If this is you restrained, I can't imagine what it's like when you cut loose. We won't need to cook again until Christmas."

"Good."

"Miss Addie said next time you're in town, you better come in to see her."

"I should have gone in today, but if I had, we'd be there for hours. We have to get back to the ranch before dark."

His gaze shifted to the dash clock. "If traffic is light, we'll make it. You should call Madison and give her an update."

Maggie reached for her purse. "Paul first. I want to know if he's popped the question." Her stomach fluttered. "Della will say yes, won't she? I mean, they look happy."

"They are. But when have you seen them?"

"In the photos on the piano." Maggie frowned. "You know my parents were crazy about each other, but Paul and me, well, we were mostly inconvenient."

"You've told me they weren't exactly candidates for parents of the year."

"No, they weren't that." She let out a humorless laugh. "They did what was necessary but we were outsiders. Their world was closed to the two of them." If not for Paul, she'd have thought that was her fault. He made sure she knew it was just their way. "It's bothered me for a long time that my parents never took photos of Paul. When I got old enough, I did, but there were dozens of me that he took and only a few of him. Now the whole piano top is covered with photos of him and Della and Uncle Warny and me. I love that."

"You love seeing Paul happy."

"I do." Her brother had made her being happy his priority in life. She was grateful for his sacrifices and the care he'd taken to make sure she'd grown up secure and loved.

"Don't worry. She'll say yes. Della Jackson is head over heels in love with your brother." Ian gave Maggie's hand a reassuring squeeze. "You're a good sister."

"I'm not. But I am so glad about Della. On the phone it's hard to tell, and it's really important to me that Paul be loved." She craved that for him. "You know that without him my childhood would have been miserable, right? But it wasn't. He made it magical."

"Your parents were here."

"Even when they lived here, they weren't here, Ian. Well, not for Paul and me."

Ian stiffened. "I heard they flew in after the Utah incident." When she nodded, he added, "Did they really go back to Costa Rica while you were still in ICU and Paul was in the hospital?"

She nodded again. "Paul was banged up pretty badly and I was clinging to life by a thread, but as soon as Uncle Warny arrived, they said he would watch over us. They had to get home." Her tight jaw quivered. Maybe he wouldn't notice. "Commitments, you know."

"I thought they had an emergency." Ian looked over at her.

"They did. Their social schedule had been disrupted for a week. For them, that's an emergency." Her resentment of that—their social activities rating higher with them than Paul and her—reverberated in her voice. She didn't bother to try to hide it. The minute she left for college, they had taken off to Costa Rica. They'd vacationed there many times and loved it.

"I'm so sorry. I had no idea."

"Family secret. No one knew, or ever did, though Madison figured it out. When we were kids, she was always at the ranch. Paul couldn't hide the truth from her, but he saw to it that no one else knew. I'm still not sure why he covered for them, but he did."

"If you were profiling, what would you conclude?" Ian turned off the radio. "I'd think he'd be angry and bitter and let everyone know."

"If it had been just him, he might have. But—it took me a while to figure this out—Paul didn't do anything for them. He did everything he did for me. My darling brother didn't want me to feel as if I wasn't loved or that my own parents didn't care about me."

"Makes sense, yet I'm hearing a but in your voice."

"You are astute, Dr. Crane. There is a but." She warbled her eyebrows. "The truth is, they didn't love or care about either of us. Paul and I were tolerated. Our parents pulled us off the shelf when it was convenient and shoved us back on it when it wasn't. It mostly wasn't." She swiped her hair back from her face. "I was lucky. Paul made sure I had all the love and support in the world. He was the one who did without—at least, until Uncle Warny showed up. Paul was in his teens then." A lump rose in her throat. "That's why it's so important to me that he be happy now."

"You love him."

"I do. I'm ashamed to say it, but for years I had no idea no one else loved him. I was little and clueless, but once I realized that…" Her throat again thickened, and her voice grew husky. "Well, I've tried to let him know ever since."

Ian flashed her an enigmatic smile. "Between you and Della, I'd say that you can rest easy. He's loved by two special women. That makes him a lucky man."

"Is Della a hugger?" Maggie asked, relieved and curious and eager to learn more. "I'm a hugger. Paul's a big hugger. He needs hugs."

"She's a hugger." Ian smiled. "I am, too—just for the record."

"I know. You even hug with your voice."

"Excuse me?" He turned off the pavement and onto the ranch road. Plumes of dust rose up behind him.

"When we talk on the phone. You hug me with your voice. It's lovely."

A strange look she couldn't interpret flashed across his face. He stopped the SUV at the gate, punched in the code and then ran through the biometric scan.

The broad black metal gate swung open.

Maggie watched to make sure it closed all the way behind them. When it had, she pivoted to look ahead. What she expected to see wasn't there. Where was Jake? He always came out to meet her. And Uncle Warny? And why was Thunder still in the exercise yard? "Slow down, Ian."

He slowed to a crawl. "Why?"

"Something's wrong." Dread dragged at her belly. She pulled her weapon from her purse, scanned the pasture, the woods, between the trees and thick foliage abutting the road.

The house looked fine from the front, but as they rounded the back toward the garage and barn, Ian hit the brakes. "Oh, no."

In the broad yard near the back porch, both Jake and Uncle Warny lay on the ground.

"Leave your lights on." Darkness was settling in, overtaking dusk, and thick shadows lay everywhere. Maggie rushed out and took off running, terror spiking her already pounding pulse. They weren't moving. *Why weren't they moving?*

Flat on his back, her uncle lay with his arms crossed over his stomach, his baseball cap pulled down to shield his face.

And in his hand, he held a black rose.

"Maggie, answer me." Ian repeated. "Is he breathing?"

Shaking hard, she lifted the cap, bracing for what she might see. But Uncle Warny looked normal. *Thank You, God.* She lifted a hand, pressed her fingertips against his throat, checking his carotid, and found a pulse. "He's breathing. Is Jake?"

Ian was on the phone. "Yes, but we've got a complication."

Maggie tried to rouse her uncle. He didn't wake up, but he did snore. She did a quick first-aid scan. "He's been drugged, Ian."

"Jake, too."

She shot a look past the huge fir, twenty yards away, to where Jake lay. And why had Ian, a doctor, gone to the dog rather than to her uncle? "What's the complication?"

"There's a bomb collar on Jake's neck."

"Back away. Do it now, Ian." Panic flooded her. "Crawford loves bombs." She shouldn't have come back here. Now, he was going to kill Jake, and if Ian didn't move, he'd die with him. "Move!"

Ian sprinted over to her. "I've called out Major Beecher. He's a bomb squad specialist at the base. He and his team are on the way." He ran a quick check on Warny. "Pulse and respiration are fine." Lifting his lid, he checked one eye and then the other. "He seems okay. Drugged to the rafters but, for the moment, okay."

Relief washed through her, but her gaze slid to Jake and fear rushed right back.

Waiting for Beecher was the longest half hour of her life. "Crawford had to do this." While they'd stopped by the café to pick up food, he'd made a beeline from the cemetery to the ranch. "He'll wait until the last minute, you know." On the ground beside her uncle, she held his hand and fixated on Jake. "That's what he does. He waits and waits until you think you're going to make it, and then, boom, he strikes. Your world explodes and nothing is ever again the same."

"Let's hope not."

"Paul loves that dog. So do I." She couldn't cry, she

couldn't allow herself to be that weak. She had to be strong, detached and to think. "Why did I come home? This is my fault. If I'd just kept running—"

"You'd be dead, Maggie. He would have caught you in Nashville and we'd be responding to the call telling us they'd found your body." Ian's voice was flat and firm. "You didn't collar or drug Jake or Warny or put that rose in his hands." Ian looked to where the rose lay in the grass beside Warny's hip.

"No, but I knew he would come after me. I knew he'd follow me home, and I came back anyway. That was a selfish, stupid thing to do."

"Getting yourself killed would have been a stupid thing to do. Coming home was smart, your last resort."

She repeated that to herself over and again, trying to convince herself it was so, determined to believe it. But if it was true, why didn't it rouse that sense of knowing in her that it was? Why did it feel so self-serving and hollow and empty?

Finally Beecher and his two-man team arrived, diverting her attention from her guilt and misery. Dressed in bomb gear, they got a grip on the situation from Ian, and then approached the dog. Jake still lay unconscious, as motionless as he'd been since they'd found him. Beecher examined the device, the team mumbled among themselves, and then Beecher removed his headgear. "It's not hot."

Clammy and shaking, Maggie shuddered a deep sigh of relief. Her whole body collapsed inside as if pounded boneless and limp. "He'll be okay then?"

Beecher removed the collar, took another intense look at it. "He'll be fine." He lifted something off the ground and tucked it into a clear evidence bag and then tucked the bag into his pocket. Looking to the first of the other two on his team, he issued the order. "Thompson, go check Warny."

"Yes sir, Major." He double-timed it over to Maggie, dropped down and began running through emergency medical procedures. He pulled blood and did some field test with a smear.

"Can you tell what it is?" Maggie asked.

"Not without a thorough toxicology, but my best guess is it's a common sedative." He spared her a glance. "I've seen results like this before."

"Ian's a doctor," Maggie said, glancing at him pacing a short distance away. He was reporting in to Detective Cray—and likely to Madison and Paul, though Maggie hoped not, since they were stuck where they were. No sense in worrying them even more about something they couldn't do a thing about. "He says they were sedated, too."

"We'll know with what when I get the reports." Thompson rolled Uncle Warny over onto his side. He stopped snoring and his eyes fluttered open.

"Maggie?"

Relief gushed through her. "Yes, Uncle Warny?"

"This ground's hard."

"Yes, it is."

He squinted up at her. The beam of light from Beecher's response vehicle's headlights sliced over his body. "Why am I on it?"

Pushing herself, she forced her tone light, hoping he'd take a cue from her and stay calm. "Apparently you decided to take a nap."

"I'm sure as certain I did not. I was exercising Thunder—and it was morning, now it's not."

"He's fine," Thompson said, and then reached into his black case for something she couldn't see.

Maybe, but he looked droopy-eyed and confused. "How'd I get here?" Uncle Warny asked her.

Maggie stroked his rugged face. "I was hoping you could tell me that."

"Last thing I remember is holding Thunder's reins. Jake barked and...that's it." He pivoted his head and glared at Thompson. "Who are you and why are you checking my heart with a stethoscope?" He shot a hard look at his niece. "Did I have a heart attack and you're not telling me?"

"No," Maggie said. "Lieutenant Thompson is with Major Beecher. They're checking to see what happened."

"Which would be easier if you'd be still for a minute, sir." Thompson ruffled the hair low on Warny's neck. "There it is." He turned and called out, "Major Beecher, I found the entry-point wound."

Beecher joined them, stared at a little red pinpoint of blood dotting the back of Uncle Warny's neck. Darkness settled in, and he pulled a flashlight from a zippered pants pocket and shined its beam on Uncle Warny's neck. "Get a few photos."

Thompson snapped a few shots with his cell phone, then stowed it in his pocket.

Beecher frowned at Maggie. "The good news is he'll sleep tonight and most of tomorrow, but there shouldn't be any long-term residual affects."

How could he know that about residual effects from a single prick-point of blood? "What are you seeing on his neck that I'm not?"

Beecher held her gaze and lowered his voice so only the two of them could hear. "Something I've seen many times but I've never seen used against Americans on

American soil. I can't say anything more than that. I can say there is some bad news."

Ian stood within hearing distance, but pretended to be as deaf as a stone and he avoided her eyes. He knew what had been used on Uncle Warny and Jake and he was as gagged as Beecher and unable to tell her. That could be for only one reason. Whatever had been used had *military application* written all over it. What else could warrant a gag order on Beecher *and* Ian? He'd been a civilian for over three— Ah, wait. Beecher hadn't deduced residual effects just from the pinprick on her uncle's neck. It'd been that *and* whatever he'd picked up and stashed in his pocket in that evidence bag. "What's the bad news?" she asked Beecher.

"Whoever did this is a professional with access to assets not typically seen in the civilian sector."

Definitely military assets. Talbot or Dayton? Her gaze locked with Ian's, asking the unspoken question.

"Not necessarily," Ian said, brushing at the grass clinging to his knees. Nightfall had taken hold and only the light from the headlamps in the SUV and in Beecher's response vehicle lit the dark. The tall fir rustled off her right shoulder, and the brisk wind ruffled Ian's hair. "Production and manufacturing are handled by civilians."

Maggie processed that. Crawford could have bought it, stolen it or hired on somewhere to get personal access. With the Black Beauty rose, Crawford had to have done this.

Uncle Warny grunted. "Maggie girl, could you get me off this cold ground. My bones are about frozen solid."

Ian and Maggie flanked him and helped him up. "Ian," Warny said, "can you get Thunder into the barn?

He's gonna be stiffer than a rigor corpse, being out in the cold this long."

"Go on, Ian. I'll get Uncle Warny inside." She looked beyond him to Beecher. "Would you carry Jake for me? His bed is in the kitchen."

"Sure, Maggie." Beecher's forehead crinkled in a deep frown. "We've been briefed on what you've been through for the past three and a half years. I'm sorry that after all that you're having a lousy homecoming."

Not half as sorry as she was. Of course, she was the reason it was lousy. She shouldn't be here. Exactly what she had feared would happen was happening. She had to fix that.

And to pray hard Crawford wouldn't keep coming after her family anyway.

Standing in his Rhino ATV on the far side of the creek, he watched the activity near the ranch house through the binoculars.

He knew every inch of this property. Knew all about the security and surveillance—the Mason land was under camera observation 24/7. But provided he didn't get careless or do anything stupid, the only ones who'd know he had been here were the birds and squirrels. He'd been preparing for this day for a long time, a contingency to his contingency plan, though honestly he had hoped not to be forced into implementing it. Few would believe it, but he actually liked Maggie Mason. He respected her courage and the lengths she would go to, to protect her family.

Something he couldn't say for his own.

As long as she stayed away from North Bay, everything had been fine. He'd monitored every email she'd saved as a draft, every one she'd sent, and listened to every phone conversation she had. Her switching phones hadn't created even a minor blip. As soon as she reported in, he had her. He'd gotten to know her very well in the past three-plus years. The constant exposure to what she said and wrote made it easy to determine the way she thought, her strengths and weaknesses, and likes and dislikes. Without giving him that advantage, she might have caught him. She was sharp, quick and blunt and honest. Rare traits in women—at least, in the women in his life. He loved testing her, pushing her to the limits to see how she'd react. Impressive. Very impressive. But then she'd ruined it all. She'd come back home and that…changed everything.

She had been so caught up in the cat-and-mouse game she hadn't realized there was more she knew that Crane didn't know. Information about his wife's activities at the time of her death that, in his hands, could be problematic.

Now she had shared it, and she and Crane were acting on that information together.

That, coupled with finding a printed email draft from Maggie to Crane at Crane's house, had forced his hand. She was even better than he'd thought. Setting up a fake email account. Never transmitting messages through it. Just the two of them signing in to it under the same ID and password, reading drafts. He hadn't expected her to adopt terrorist tactics, and he should have anticipated the possibility. That he hadn't even considered it annoyed him. She was the mouse, not the cat. The hunted, not the hunter. But apparently she hadn't gotten the memo on that. She pursued as often as she was pursued, and she'd gotten far too close.

Dangerously close.

Then she'd come home. Anger churned in his stomach. At the airport in Nashville, he'd modified his plan. David Pace had to go. His records and Beth's had to be destroyed. Ian Crane definitely had to go. And, of course, now Maggie had to go, too.

He doubted that news would surprise her. She'd documented in one of her FBI reports the aversion to loose ends, and from the body of knowledge she'd generated on her adversary, she had to know that the time for game playing was done. Even if she hadn't drawn that conclusion on her own, she had been given fair warning. The roses said it all.

Black Beauty roses. Rare and, like him, not found in nature but created by man. They symbolized death, impending doom and a perilous journey, which, of course, was why they had been chosen. She knew that—she'd looked it up. Just as she knew that they also symbolized distaste or disdain between rivals, which is why they'd been chosen specifically for her. Most of the killings weren't acrimonious. Her adversary simply liked to kill. But there were exceptions, and those exceptions were always warned. Like his second victim.

Authorities thought only his second victim and Maggie had gotten the single roses. But Maggie actually was the fourth, and she'd been gifted with several. Yes, indeed. She'd been entertaining, very resourceful, particularly for a woman he'd once severely injured and kept under duress. Yet the season for play, like all seasons, had to end so a new season could begin.

The killing season.

Still, he would miss her—and that likely would surprise her.

He watched her walk the old man into the house through the back door.

Five days. Start your Christmas countdown now, Maggie. Don't delay.

In five days, you'll be dead.

SIX

After dinner, Warny went upstairs to Paul's room and within minutes was sawing logs. Jake hadn't awakened long enough to eat, only to get a dog treat left for him on the floor near his bed, and he crashed again before he got half of it down. He was snoring, too, though not nearly as loud as Warny.

Ian and Maggie cleaned up the kitchen. She worked quickly, efficiently, and mindful of Dayton's warning, Ian watched her for signs of PTSD but saw none. She seemed calm and, for all purposes, normal—far more normal than he. Every nerve in his body was raw and snapping. He was edgy and on full alert. The last time he'd felt like this he'd been in the zone in Afghanistan. But Maggie acted as if it were a normal day. She'd eaten well, talked with Paul and Della and then with Madison, and she'd even joked with them. How she did it, knowing Crawford was in North Bay or close by, Ian had no idea.

Now she had the tabletop covered with ingredients— powdered sugar, eggs, boxes of graham crackers and bags of gumdrops, candy canes and peppermint rounds. "What are you doing?"

"Making a gingerbread house." She wrapped a tray

in shiny foil and smoothed it down, crimping the edges around the tray. "I usually make the gingerbread, but it's been a rough day. Graham crackers will have to do this year." She stuffed icing in a Ziploc bag with a plastic tip punching through its bottom corner, and then beaded a line of it to glue together two crackers. "When I was little, Paul and I used graham crackers for the walls and roof all the time." A hint of a smile curved her lips. "I wasn't yet allowed to use the stove." She glanced up at him. "Can you hold that wall up so I can put the roof on?"

Ian stretched over and held the wall crackers vertical. "Maggie, are you in denial?"

"About what?"

"Crawford."

She paused, and then started buttering icing onto the next cracker, shingling the roof. "He's impossible to deny, don't you think?"

"I do, which is why I'm wondering how you're managing to act so normal, when today has been anything but. First the connection with Beth and David Pace, then Brett Lund killing himself, and then Crawford or Blue Shoes—*somebody*—taking a shot at us. We could have been killed today but—"

"We weren't."

"But we could have been."

"Ah, I see." She bit into her lower lip, focusing on attaching the first of the roof crackers. "Dayton was wrong. I don't have PTSD, Ian. After Utah, I had to get a psych evaluation before I returned to active duty." She pressed the cracker down, reached into the package for another and then buttered it. "I guess it does seem odd to you that I can feel normal or do normal things, but it's not odd to me." She paused, the knife midair, and looked at him. "When you live like I've been living, you take the good whenever you can find it, and when a crisis is over, you let go of it. You assess and see where you were weak, seek ways to strengthen, and then put it on the back burner where it belongs."

"So fast?" She made sense, but he had doubts. "How do you process so much in such a condensed period of time? You're moving at warp speed."

"I have no choice. It's cope and deal with it…at warp speed…or get run over."

"Run over?"

"It's harder to hit a moving target, Ian. If you don't move on quickly, you won't be prepared when the next crisis hits. You'll still be looking back instead of ahead." She adjusted another roof shingle. "Don't military doctors take tactical training?"

"Yes, but even in it, processing took days, sometimes weeks."

"Do that with Crawford, and you'll only need to do it once. While you're processing, he'll be killing you."

Her time alone had been horrific. He'd known it, and she'd been open in discussing some of her trials and challenges, but he hadn't grasped her situation having impacts like this. "Do you think Crawford will come here again?"

"I think he'll strike again. But whether or not it'll be here, I don't know. No history on that. Typically, I'd be running again now." She reached for another cracker. Seamed it into place. "I haven't had such a close encounter and stayed put." She opened a new package of crackers. The cellophane crackled. "I shouldn't stay put now."

His chest went tight, his stomach knotted. "Don't you dare run on me, Maggie."

"I'm not." She slid a long cracker out of the torn

package. "I considered it, but without a guarantee he'd leave Uncle Warny and you alone, I can't." She put the last cracker on the roof. "That die was cast when I came home." She blinked then stood to put the *"snow"* on the roof. "I regret it now, but done is done, and—"

"Things are what they are." She wouldn't run. Should he be happy or more worried? Unsure, he watched her work.

"Why don't you check the security monitors then prepare to gumdrop?" She shot him a warning look. "I put the candy canes around the door."

He smiled. He couldn't help it. "How about you put one on the left, and I'll do the one on the right?"

She twisted her mouth, tilted her head. "I guess we could negotiate. But it's going to cost you. I've always done the candy canes."

"Oh-oh. Negotiate. I've seen you do that. It's not pretty." He rubbed his jaw. "What are the damages apt to run? I have a feeling I'm going to get soaked or hosed or worse."

"Oh, you are." She grinned. "We'll start with you telling me about your Christmases when you were young and see if that's worth amending the tradition."

Pleasantly surprised, he grunted. "I can handle that." He went to check the monitors. In a ten-by-ten room just off the kitchen near the back door, they covered an entire wall. He studied each of them, saw one oddity but nothing out of the ordinary, and then returned to the kitchen.

"Everything looks okay," he told her. "But I'm curious about that clearing on the far side of the pasture— the one on the hill near the creek."

"Because it's clear and the rest we keep natural?"

He nodded.

"I cleared it." A wistful look crossed her face. "I was getting ready to build a home there when all this started with Crawford."

"I'm sorry," Ian said and meant it. Maggie loved this land, and he doubted she could be content anywhere else. So she'd dreamed of building her own home here, and Crawford had stolen that from her along with everything else.

She had a pile of red gumdrops set apart from the others, and snagged one and put it in her mouth. Scooping a handful of green, yellow and orange ones, she dotted the roof. "You do the backside and tell me about your Christmases."

"They were good. Loud." He popped a green gumdrop into his mouth. "All my mom's family lived close, and everyone congregated at her mother's house. Between the kids, spouses and their kids, there must have been thirty of us, plus whatever strays Gramps brought home. He couldn't stand the thought of anyone being alone on Christmas."

"Compassionate man. As we both know, being alone on Christmas is horrible." She paused decorating the house. "You still miss him."

"I do." He'd passed away the year before Beth. "We did everything together—except play golf."

"He didn't like golf?"

"He loved it." Ian grinned. "We went to his club and played once. I was nine. The manager said he'd give Gramps a year's worth of green fees if he wouldn't bring me back."

"What did you do?" Maggie tried not to smile. "That's awful."

"It was terrific. I hated golf. Pretty much messed up their greens." His face burned. "Gramps took offense, but before he could refuse the manager's offer, I negotiated a better deal."

"He was going to leave the club." She laughed. "You fixed it where he had to stay."

"Free green fees for two years." Ian chuckled. "I got bad marks from Gramps on golf, but great ones on negotiating."

"Ian." She shook her head. "How'd you get the manager from one year to two?"

"I said I planned to get good at golf even if I had to play every day."

She laughed harder.

So did Ian.

She stopped and squeezed his hand. "I'll bet you were Gramps's favorite."

"I think at times we all were. He made time for each of us, so we had his full attention. We all felt special." Ian clasped her arm, resting on his shoulder, looked up into her smiling face and sobered. "Maggie, you've done the impossible."

"What?"

"News today about Beth, all this with Crawford and Blue Shoes, and yet you've managed to make me laugh."

"I like it." She smoothed his sleeve and backed away.

"Me, too." He stilled, leaned against the table. Guilt settled in on him. Beth was dead. Dead, and he sat here laughing. "Does that make me an awful person?"

"No, Ian. It doesn't." Maggie unwrapped a candy cane. "Do you know the story of the candy cane?"

"They used to use ribbon to decorate barbershop poles to mimic candy canes?" He shrugged. "That's the only story about them I've ever heard."

"Oh, Ian." She made a *tsk-tsk* clicking sound with

her tongue against the roof of her mouth. "You slept through Sunday school."

"We never talked about candy canes in Sunday school."

"Well, isn't that a shame?" She tilted her head. "It's a very cool story."

"So are you going to tell it to me, or do I have to run a web search?"

"I'll tell you." She unwrapped a candy cane and frosted its backside as she talked. "A candy maker created a hard white candy and shaped it like a J for Jesus. Some say it's used to shepherd the lost and, when they go astray, He hooks them and brings them back into the fold, so they call it a Shepherd's hook." She pressed the candy cane into place, framing the left side of the doorway on the gingerbread house. "Its being white is a symbol for Mary and the virgin birth of Christ— pure and sinless—and the three red stripes represent two things. These two thin ones represent Christ being scourged, and the thick one is to remind us that Christ bled on the cross to give us eternal life." She studied the candy. "Some put green in them and don't stick to the traditional three red stripes, but I don't buy those. The stripes have important meanings, so I always look for those that follow the tradition." She passed him the second candy cane.

Knowing now how important placing the candy canes were to her, Ian paused then drew back his hand. "No, you go ahead."

She smiled, lifted his hand and placed the candy cane gently in his palm. "Frame the doorway, Ian. If you frame it, you know it's there, and then you can walk through."

His mouth went dry. This symbolized far more than

the doorway to a gingerbread house. It symbolized acknowledging God's place in his life. He believed; he'd always believed. But from the time of Beth's death until now, he'd been angry with God, blamed Him for allowing her death. Yet in the simple story of a candy cane, he recalled how much Christ suffered, and it made him feel petty and small. Remorseful and contrite, too. It reminded him how much he was loved and how great a sacrifice had been made for him. His heart beat fast and hard and his pulse throbbed in his ears. *I owe You an apology.* "Don't let me mess it up," he told Maggie.

"You won't," she promised. "You can't mess it up."

He seated the candy cane to the right of the door, positioned it just so, nudged it a tad, then sat back to take a look. "Is that right?"

At his side, she bent down and eyed it. "Perfect."

Maybe she was overly stressed anyway. "Maggie, it's not perfect. The whole gingerbread house is listing twenty degrees. The snow on the roof would be heavier on the north side than the south, you ate all the red gumdrops, and my candy cane is stuck on crooked."

She laughed and hugged him hard. "Not the gingerbread house, Ian. You." He smelled so good, like soap and fresh air, and the urge to kiss him hit her suddenly and hard. Before she could stop and talk herself out of it, she kissed him, stunning them both, and started to pull away.

Ian pulled her closer, cradled her against his chest and kissed her again.

A long moment later, he looked deeply into her eyes and whispered, "I'll never again look at a candy cane and not remember your story."

"I know." She stroked his face. "Gauging by your expression, I'd say you'll remember a lot more than that."

Too tender! He shielded himself from his response to her remark, and added, "I'll never again see a gingerbread house without remembering tonight, either." He studied her eyes, the gentleness in them. "I have a whole new appreciation for your traditions."

"So do I."

Her cell phone rang and she sobered, stepping over to the kitchen bar and answering with it on speakerphone. "Hello."

"You can run. You cannot hide."

Maggie shot a look at the clock on the stove. Straight-up midnight. "Coward." She punched the disconnect button.

Ian stood, joining her at the counter. "What was that about?"

Dread flooded her eyes. "It means, in this game of cat and mouse, I'm the mouse."

"It was Crawford." Ian frowned.

She shrugged. "We knew he was here."

"We suspected it. Him, Blue Shoes, one and the same or a copycat—we had a lot of possibilities. But now we know it's him." Ian reached for the phone. "I'll call Detective Cray."

"You can call him, but it's a waste of time. I've run locators on every phone call like that I've gotten. Some are near wherever I am. But many of the others, especially lately, have been from bizarre places—Iceland, Germany, Iraq. Places I know he can't be."

Ian stilled.

Maggie noticed. "What?"

"We have contact points in all those places."

She leaned a hip against the kitchen counter. "Contact points? What are you saying?"

This development wasn't what he'd hoped to find.

It was his worst nightmare. "I'm saying, run the locator on this call."

"I guess you'll get around to telling me what's on your mind soon enough." She phoned the call in to the agency, made her request and then waited for a woman to process it.

Finally she came back on the line. "Fussa."

"Fussa? Where is that?" Maggie asked.

"In the Tama area."

Ian offered his answer. "Western Tokyo."

"Add it to the interim report, will you? I'll submit the final later. Thanks." Maggie hung up. "Tokyo. See what I mean? It's crazy. He can't drug my uncle and Jake and then a few hours later be on the ground in Tokyo. It's not physically possible."

"No, it's not." Ian pulled out his phone.

"What are you doing?"

"Following a hunch." Ian got online on his iPad and keyed in a search. In short order, he sucked in a sharp breath. "Yokota is there."

"What's a Yokota?"

"A military base." Ian let her see his worry. "All the other non-local-to-you places you've been called from— do you have a list?"

"Yeah."

"Get it," Ian said.

She parked a hand on her hip. "Are you going to tell me what you're on to here?"

"I think we're going to find all of the nonlocal locations of these calls are ones with U.S. military installations."

"You are aware that I do profiling consults with the military."

"That's the only way you'd know about the Nest."

He nodded. "But those consults explain you calling others. It doesn't explain Crawford calling you from those locations—"

"You think he's somehow routing the calls through the installations." She slapped her forehead. "I can't believe I didn't pick up on that before now."

"We don't know it yet."

"I know it. Crawford's not tracking me through the FBI—we thought there could be a leak there. He's tracking me through my military connections. But how?"

"Have you been keeping them *and* the agency informed of your whereabouts?"

She nodded. "Have to or I'd lose my security clearances, and without those I can't get anything done."

"Okay." Ian stood up, paced between the granite bar and the table, his reflection catching in the polished surface. "Then this development raises a question we need to answer. How is Crawford gaining access to military routers? Is he military? A civilian contractor? A consultant? Is he in the Intelligence realm? He can't just be hacking into their phone systems. There's got to be a legitimate connection or they'd have shut him down long ago. They haven't. And that raises another question."

"What other question?"

"Is Crawford really Crawford?" Ian looked her right in the eye. "Or is he Mr. Blue Shoes pretending to be Crawford?"

"Or Crawford pretending to be Mr. Blue Shoes."

Ian stilled, parked a hand at his hip. "Maybe they are one and the same."

The next morning, Maggie and Ian had breakfast with Uncle Warny and then he left the table. "I'm going to the barn to check on Thunder. If he's half as stiff as

I am this morning, poor fella's gonna need extra walking time to loosen up."

When he'd gone, Maggie and Ian verified the listing of call locations. Not one location lacked a military facility, and while the agency couldn't trace the calls specifically to the facilities, common sense led her boss to the same conclusion it had them.

Maggie reported their findings to the task force handling the Crawford cases but withheld military notification. If General Talbot or Colonel Dayton were involved, the last thing they needed to know was that she and Ian had made the military connection.

Ian again checked the monitors and rejoined Maggie when she got off the phone. "Madison," Maggie told him, "thinks Crawford could be military. She doesn't think he and Blue Shoes are the same person because Crawford has been too actively engaged in trying to kill me. They've been tied up with their duties here."

"Doesn't mean they aren't sending an emissary, who might or might not know who he or she is working for, Maggie." Ian poured himself a fresh cup of coffee.

"Maggie!" Uncle Warny came rushing in with Jake fast on his heels. "Somebody's been messing with your car."

She stood up. "What do you mean?"

"There's flowers on it. I'm supposing you didn't put 'em there." His face looked piqued. "I went out to walk Thunder and saw 'em strewn out all over the thing—roof, hood, everywhere."

"Black roses?" she asked, her heart racing.

"Yup." His chest heaved.

"You sit down and rest up, Uncle Warny." She reached for her handbag, retrieved her weapon. "Don't you go out there, Maggie girl. Wait for the police."

"I can't wait. He could be setting bombs. We have the horses, the barns, our vehicles. The longer we wait, the more danger we're in."

"She's right." Ian met her at the back door. "Keep it locked, Warny, and keep Jake with you."

The old man nodded. "Watch out for her, son."

It was cold out. Gray and dismal. Maggie's breath frosted the air. She lifted the front of her sweater to cover her mouth and muffle her exhaling from view. The huge fir stood strong and green in the middle of the yard. It'd always been her favorite tree. She'd had tea parties near its broad base, and played dolls there and played ball with Paul. Before she'd left here, they'd decorated it for Christmas every year. If there was time, it'd be a good project for her and Ian.

She scanned the pasture, then the woods and finally the bank of the creek. No reflections of anything shiny or any mirror, no sounds of any four-wheeler, or signs of movement beyond a few squirrels.

Ian joined her at the fir. "I don't see a thing out of place."

She looked across the expanse between them and the garage. The barn was beside it. The animals didn't sound disturbed. That helped settle her nerves.

Ian stepped out into the open, walked closer to her car.

"Stay away from it. Crawford loves to bomb cars."

"I know." He kept moving.

She caught up to him, checking her peripheral. The cold had her eyes watering, but still no odd sounds intruded. No strange movements caught her eye. The wind crept over them, as if it, too, remained guarded. The black roses lay on the hood, the top, the trunk. "He was here."

"He's gone now."

"Yes." She had to agree. She sensed nothing, and with her honed instincts and Ian's in agreement, she felt certain he was long gone. But that he had been on the ranch again and the security cameras hadn't picked him up had her insides quivering like gelatin. Jake hadn't barked. The horses hadn't whinnied. No alarm had triggered. That was just odd. Jake could still be off from the sedative, but the horses? Paul's stellar security system? The only explanation was that Crawford had come onto the land through the woods and creek rather than through the road or gate.

"What?"

She couldn't make herself look away. So many roses. "He's never done this before."

"Done what?" Ian still held his gun in his hand, but reached up and zipped his jacket.

"Put so many roses in one place. He usually just leaves one."

Ian stepped into her line of vision. "Do you think the number is significant?"

"It is to him." She finally broke her gaze and looked at Ian. "But how? I have no idea."

"What is his pattern?"

"One to his second victim. One to me twice in the past, then one in Illinois on the porch. One at the cemetery on the back of Beth's grave, one on that dud device he put on Jake and one in Uncle Warny's hand. That's a total of seven. All single roses." She mentally shifted through his file, his habits, taking another view on the obvious and the subtle. "This just doesn't fit, Ian."

"Wait." He inched a little closer to the car. "They're not all roses. They're petals."

Dread dragged at Maggie. "Count the stems." She

couldn't see those on top of the car. Being taller, Ian could.

"Four stems." He backed away from the car, returned to Maggie. "Eleven roses."

"Definitely doesn't fit." She looked up at him. "Let's get out of the open. You can't trust that he isn't within shooting distance."

They returned the way they'd come, hugging the house to the fir by the creek, then back through the opening to the back door.

Inside, Ian holstered his gun at the small of his back then peeled off his jacket and hung it on an unused hook.

"Everything okay?" Warny yelled out.

"Except Crawford's been here," Maggie called back. "We saw no sign of him, though."

Maggie put her jacket on the hook beside Ian's. Their sleeves touched. She liked the way they looked side by side. She shouldn't. But she did. Just as she shouldn't like him putting himself in danger to look at the car with her. When you've seen the carnage Crawford's left in his wake, facing him without fear is impossible. Yet having Ian with her helped. At least, it did in one way. She wasn't facing the monster alone. In another way, it made it harder. She endangered Ian, and she shouldn't rely on him in ways that demanded he risk his life. He didn't owe her that kind of loyalty.

"Glad to hear that varmint ain't on the ranch." Warny shuffled toward the door.

"No." Maggie blocked his path. "You can't go out there right now."

"Why not? You said he ain't here."

"I said we didn't see him. He's a marksman. He could be a long way away and still shoot."

Ian interceded. "I've called Cray. He's sending a unit out to take the statement and Beecher is coming to run a bomb check."

Maggie frowned. "Poor guys are getting a workout with us, aren't they?"

"His team's clocking in hours on readiness training. Beecher's fine with it, Maggie. Cray's probably chugging antacid."

"Can't blame him for that." She washed her hands at the sink. Squirted soap and rubbed them hard, turned the tap so the water was as hot as she could stand it. Any time Crawford was involved or close she had that icky slimy feeling. It wasn't logical, of course, but it was relentless.

Ian grabbed an apple from the bowl of fruit on the counter. "You said that this doesn't fit Crawford's pattern. Why?"

"In the past, he's always only left one rose until after his victims were dead. Then he's had a dozen delivered to their graves. Until today, he's never left multiple roses, or given anyone living more than one."

"Maybe he don't see you as a victim, Maggie girl." Uncle Warny rubbed at his neck.

"If he didn't, he wouldn't have given me a rose at all." She tilted her head, snagged a bite of Ian's apple. "Crawford just doesn't breach patterns. He works in consistent numbers. Some would say he's crazy, but he's not. He just has a very different way of seeing and processing things. To him, his reasoning is clear and logical, and through four killings, he's remained consistent and methodical." She searched her mind. "He could be waiting to deliver the twelfth rose after he kills me. That would be in line with his patterns, but to leave multiple stems on the car…that doesn't fit."

"What does the twelfth rose mean—when he delivers 'em to the graveyard?"

"That he's done," Maggie said. "I'm almost positive now it means he's completed his mission and saved them."

"Saved 'em?" Uncle Warny's eyes stretched wide. "But his victims are dead and buried."

"I know." Maggie pursed her lips. "I'm not sure why—the specific reasoning varies case to case—but to him, he isn't killing these people just to kill them. In his twisted mind, he's protecting them from fates worse than death. Death is their escape. So to him, he's saving them."

"He's out of his mind."

"Yes, he is." Maggie rubbed her face. "It's kind of like a cracked mirror, Uncle Warny. You still see everything in it, but not in the same way you do when the mirror is intact."

Ian looked more disturbed. He finished the apple. Tossed the core. "So he deliberately breaks the pattern and he's not saving the last rose until he—I can't say kills you, Maggie. I just can't." Ian shuddered. "Then what else is he doing? What else could the twelfth rose mean?"

"Maybe it's a different signal or a sign of some other sort. That'd be consistent with him." Maggie looked from Jake, napping on his bed, back to Ian. "Maybe he's signaling there's something else to be found."

Warny grunted. "Or someone." He slid his gaze to Maggie.

"I'll check with the agency," Maggie went for her cell. "Make sure we don't have another victim."

Ian nodded toward the security room. "I'll check the surveillance tapes."

* * *

Thirty minutes before midnight, Maggie started tensing up. If Crawford had been signaling there was something else to find with the absence of the twelfth rose, he'd surely phone to jab at her for not finding it—whatever it happened to be.

It wasn't another victim. At least, not insofar as the agency could tell. No reports had come in, and considering the weather socking in nearly everyone in the entire country, that didn't surprise her.

"You're pretty deep in thought there."

Maggie sat in the living room, staring at the empty corner where the tree should be. She started at the sound of the man's voice, then recognized it as Ian's and smiled up at him. "Waiting for the other shoe to drop."

"The midnight call?" He sat down beside her.

She nodded. "The agency had nothing to report. Neither did my military liaison."

"I didn't see anything on the tapes, either." Ian lifted her hand, gave it a reassuring squeeze. "Maybe the missing rose wasn't a signal."

"Oh, it was, Ian." She looked over at him, his warm breath fanning her face. "I just don't yet know for what."

They ran through some possibilities and then some outside possibilities, but found nothing.

Ian frowned. "Why do you keep staring at that corner of the room?"

"The tree should be there. It's not." She gave him a bittersweet smile. "I guess I just wanted…"

"The kind of Christmas you've had at home in the past? Before Crawford?"

He always understood. She nodded. "There's no tree, no decorations inside or outside. Paul and I always strung lights on the bushes out front and framed the porch and wrapped lights around the columns. We did the back porch, too, and decorated the big fir tree in the yard. This year…nothing is decked out for Christmas."

"The table is," Ian said softly. "The gingerbread house is there."

"Yes, it is." She leaned her head against his shoulder. "I'm being silly."

He hooked her chin with his thumb, stroked it and looked deeply into her eyes. "No, Maggie. You're many things, but you're not silly."

He was going to kiss her. She saw it in his eyes, felt it in the slight tremble in his hand. Could he hear her heart racing? Could he see how much she wanted his kiss?

She tilted her face into his hand.

"Maggie?"

"Mmm?" Words were beyond her.

"I need to kiss you." His fingertips grew gentler still. "I know you don't want me to, and I shouldn't want to, but I do and…I'm going to kiss you, Maggie."

Before he could change his mind, she turned and their lips met, caressed. No gentle kiss, this. This kiss claimed and then consumed, spoke of longing and wanting and loving. Spoke of emotions felt to the core but unexpressed in years of notes and cards and calls that lasted hours and filled dark, empty nights. This kiss bombarded the senses, the emotions, and bonded souls, and when it ended, it left them breathless and staggering, wrapped in each other's arms and feeling that it was there they belonged.

He looked into her eyes. "I won't apologize."

"I'd be devastated if you did."

"I won't feel guilty, either." He stroked her hair back from her face.

"There's no need, Ian." She looked up at him, forced

her voice steady. "We both loved Beth. She's gone now, but we're not. I can't believe she wouldn't want us to be…" A worry flitted through Maggie's mind and took root. "Is this about me, or because I was close to Beth?" She didn't want to think it could be about Beth, but until he'd kissed her, she'd seriously doubted Ian was ready to move on. In fact, she'd been certain he wouldn't be ready to move on until he solved Beth's murder. Was she setting herself up for heartbreak? Oh, after all they'd both been through, the last thing either of them needed was heartbreak. This could be about Beth. Because Maggie mourned her, too. Because they'd shared that grief and those bonds. Was it? How could she know for sure?

His expression clouded. "It's about us—you and me."

"Are you sure?" He sounded sure, but was he really?

He hesitated a second. Just long enough to raise doubt. "Yes, I'm sure."

He didn't sound sure. He wasn't. How could he be? She had doubts. Surely his were stronger. But he thought he was sure, which definitely made him not sure.

He let out a frustrated sigh. "I have real feelings for you and they're deep. I never thought I'd feel this way about a woman again."

Was it her, or the memories of Beth he relived through her? That had to be it. Had to be. Her heart squeezed, a hard ache filling it. "You don't want to hurt me, I know that. But we've always been honest with each other, so I have to ask. Are you being honest with yourself?"

"I care about you. A lot. You've no idea how much. That isn't new, but it's different, too, and feeling as if it's all right to express the difference…that's new."

"Since the cemetery?" Maggie was getting a grip on this. "Since we went to Beth's grave?"

He nodded. "And since you reminded me she didn't need me anymore."

"Ian, that doesn't mean you need me." A substitute? A lump rose in her throat. Constantly compared with the love of his life? No, she couldn't do that. With Crawford, she shouldn't do anything. And she shouldn't forget it.

"It's not like that." He frowned. "Look, I might not have it all figured out yet—what this is growing between us—but I know what it isn't, and it isn't that. I do need you, Maggie."

She shouldn't push. She really shouldn't push. "Because..."

"Because you make me feel again."

She brushed the backs of her fingers along his jaw. "What do I make you feel?"

No hint of a smile touched his lips or his eyes. Nothing but a serious, sober, almost regretful pleading he couldn't verbalize. "Everything."

This wasn't about Beth. The truth came as clearly as Christmas. "You make me feel, too. You shouldn't. Not because of Beth. I believe she'd want us happy and I think she'd be glad if we could be happy together." Beth would want them to be loved.

Ian had loved Maggie for a long time. It had been clear in everything he had said and done. She'd loved him, too. She thought about it, and she was right. But it was different now in a way that probably made them both kind of panic. There was a big difference in loving and being in love. Were they falling in love? Was that the difference? What was happening?

She didn't dare ask. With Crawford, she couldn't help but not be okay with falling in love.

Ian looked at her, silent, his thoughts clearly as turbulent as her own. She couldn't reassure him. She couldn't reassure herself, though she wondered, what if there were no Crawford? What if it were just Ian and her living a normal life? Would them falling in love be okay then?

She grimaced. What difference did that make? That wasn't their situation.

Refusing to answer her own question, not daring to answer her own question, Maggie sighed and stood up. "You know what I think?"

"What?"

"I think we should not worry about us and what's happening. We should just trust that it'll work out like it's supposed to and we should focus on something else."

"I don't have it in me to take leaps of faith anymore, Maggie."

She blinked hard, buying time to think. Ian had to work through his anger with God and put this faith crisis behind him, but that was a journey and conflict between him and God. Only they could repair the broken trust. *Please, let it be sooner rather than later.* "I want to put up the tree and decorate the house, Ian. I want a merry Christmas."

Ian stood up. "Then let's go get a Christmas tree."

Maggie brightened. "Really?" When he nodded, she squealed and hugged him. "And shopping. I need to buy gifts and—"

"Hold on." He laughed. "We have four days."

"Three shopping days." She wrinkled her nose. "But we can start now. We'll pull the stuff out of the attic and—"

The phone rang.

Maggie checked the mantel clock. "Midnight."

"Don't answer it."

"I have to. He'll do something horrible." She retrieved her phone from the kitchen and answered. "Hello."

"Did you find the twelfth rose?"

Crawford. "Was I supposed to?" Her hand shook. She broke into a sweat.

"Not yet."

"Then I guess today was a draw."

"Hardly." He snorted. "Maggie, Maggie, Maggie. You're so predictable. Cute all bundled up in your white coat and boots, but predictable."

Panic shot through her body. She had been wearing a white coat and boots today. He'd seen her. "How does it feel to have to watch from a distance all the time, too scared to show your face?"

"Scared?" He laughed, cackled. "Trust me, Maggie. My face is the last thing you want to see."

"Quite the contrary. I'd love to see it."

"Sure you would. Through the site on your gun, maybe."

She stiffened. "That would work."

"Who knows? The opportunity might arise. For now, I have a message for you."

"A message?" She looked at Ian, confused. Crawford had never talked to her like this.

"You can run. You cannot hide."

The line went dead.

She hung up the phone, looked into Ian's expectant face. "He saw us at the cemetery or here—maybe both. He mentioned my white coat and boots."

"So he called to let you know it was him at the cemetery?"

"No, he had a message for me."

"What was it?"

"I'm the mouse." Her resentment of that showed in the way she punched the face of her phone, dialing. "Reporting it to the agency."

"You can bet he was local. The call might not be but the man was."

"Definitely." She reported the exchange, then waited for the locator to track the call.

"Sparrow?" the unidentified woman said. "He isn't local."

Maggie glanced ceilingward, resentful and confused. "Where is he?"

"NORAD."

"The NORAD that's tracking Santa?"

"One and the same."

"Where is it?"

"Colorado Springs."

"Thanks." Maggie disconnected, saw that Ian already sat at the kitchen table keying in a search on the laptop. "Petersen Air Force Base."

Maggie thought a long moment. "Maybe Talbot or Dayton is pretending to be Crawford. It'd be really convenient to do whatever and blame him for it."

"That could explain why he's breaking patterns." Ian looked over at her. "It's not really Crawford."

Logical conclusion, but her experience did have its perks, and her certainty was one of them. "That explains nothing. Crawford could be routing the calls pretending to be Talbot or Dayton. He's incredibly resourceful—and even more clever. He'd see humor and irony in framing one of them for his crimes." She let out a heartfelt sigh. "It's Crawford, Ian."

"He could be setting them up. But with the deviations from his patterns, we don't know that."

"I do." How she knew, she couldn't honestly say. But she felt it down to the marrow of her bones. "I've had years of this kind of parsing with him. Ordinarily, I'd say the only person on the planet who knows him better is his mother, but she was his first known victim. Seven years ago, two days before Christmas, he beat her to death and tied twenty pound lead weights to her feet."

"Lead weights?"

Maggie nodded. "He does that to all of them so they 'stay put.'"

"Why did he kill her?"

"If I knew the answer to that, he'd be caught and in jail." Maggie rubbed at a little pounding in her temple. "From all I've pieced together, she wasn't around much. Single mother and, according to him, a very hardworking woman."

"You'd think he'd admire that."

Had he? Had he admired her so much he killed her to spare her from having to work so hard? She'd thought so at one time, yet that never felt quite right. What was wrong in it niggled at the fringes of her mind, but it still hadn't come into focus. "It's hard to tell. He's caustic and takes sarcasm to new levels. He could love or hate her for it. I'm not sure." She rubbed her temple harder. "That's the thing with Crawford. He always double-talks and he does so in such a way that it rings true, but then he takes the opposite position and what he says still rings true."

"Is he sarcastic when he's lying or when he's being honest?"

"Random." She thought a second more. "That's deliberate, of course. Clever confusion."

"I hate it that you've been going through this for so long on your own. We've talked about it, but it's different, being with you and seeing it happen and the impact firsthand."

"It is, and it's totally selfish of me to be glad you're with me—it's definitely not in your best interest—but, forgive me, Ian. I am glad. This has been...incredibly hard."

"You're the understatement queen." Ian curled his arms around her. "What can I do?"

Inside, she shook. "You can hold me." She let him see her vulnerability. The constant fear she carried with her every minute of every day that she tried to hide from everyone else, including most often from herself. "Just hold me."

"Oh, Maggie." He opened his arms. "Come here."

She walked into them, felt them close around her. The comforting feel of his heart beating against her face. A shuddery breath escaped her. "This is better."

"Better than what?" He held her tighter, buried his face in the side of her neck.

"Being alone after he calls." She slipped her arms around Ian's waist and moved closer still. "I hate being alone after he calls."

Ian pressed a kiss to her crown and then whispered, "You're not alone anymore, Maggie. Those days are over."

They were over. But were they over for a lifetime? Or just for now?

That she couldn't answer.

Yet she had experience at living in the moment. She'd done nothing but live moment to moment for over three long years. She didn't need to know about tomorrow to appreciate his gift today. And because of her experience, she recognized that gift for the rare treasure it was, and so rather than feeling doubtful or pensive, she let the wave she did feel wash over her.

The wave of gratitude.

SEVEN

Christmas music floated up the stairs.

Startled by it, Maggie sat up in bed and heard Uncle Warny singing "The First Noel." Ian chimed in. He had a good voice. Smiling, she got up, showered quickly and dressed in jeans and a teal sweater, then rushed downstairs to the lyrics of "Jingle Bells."

At the foot of the stairs, she saw them setting the tree up in the empty space near the piano. The scent of evergreen wafted to her. She inhaled deeply, relishing it.

"Ah, Maggie girl. Morning." Uncle Warny motioned. "Come look and see if you think this scraggly bush will do for a proper Christmas tree."

She left the steps and joined them, already smiling, then examined the tree. It was perfect. Six beautiful feet of fat branches and long needles just waiting for lights and bulbs and traditional decorations.

"Well?"

"It obviously didn't come from the attic." She looked at an array of red and green plastic boxes littering the floor that held all the decorations. "Where'd it come from?"

"I picked it up this morning," Ian said. "I thought a fresh tree would help you get your merry Christmas."

Touched by that thoughtfulness, it wasn't lost on her that Ian needed a merry Christmas, too, and he certainly hadn't had one since Beth's death. They were both overdue. "Well, it's gorgeous. Naked, but gorgeous." She smiled. "I think it'll be a fabulous tree."

"I'll get some coffee for you, Maggie girl. You fight with those tangled up lights and get them on the tree."

She frowned. "You know I hate doing the lights." She sent Ian a hopeful look.

"Sorry." He shrugged, the front of his shirt dusted with flour and splatters of…something gooey. "I'm on baking duty. Snickerdoodles."

Snickerdoodles? "You're joking me."

"No, unfortunately, I'm not."

"But—" Ian didn't cook much. He never had.

"Warny shoved your grandmother's cookbook at me and said they were your favorite. If I could learn to practice medicine, I could bake a cookie. I figured he had a point, so I'm giving it a shot—and making no promises whatsoever they'll be edible."

The stove timer went off.

"That's my cue." Ian rushed from the living room to the kitchen.

Maggie followed him. "The lights can wait a minute. I need food and coffee." Looking at the total disaster in the kitchen—was every single dish used to make a batch of cookies?—she needed lots and lots of coffee.

Uncle Warny shoved a filled cup in her hands. "We had cereal this morning so we could get moving. That okay, or you need something hot?"

"Cereal's great." She took the box and then filled a bowl with something that resembled tree bark and nuts and splashed on milk. Jake was fairly dancing. "What's he so excited about?" Paul always saved Jake a bite. But dancing for tree bark? Not happening. A bone? By all means.

Uncle Warny passed her a spoon. "We've been eating the broken cookies. Getting rid of the evidence." He nodded at the breakfast bar, and lowered his voice. "Ian needed a little practice run at getting 'em off the cookie sheet and on the paper."

She glanced over. The bar was covered in wax paper with curling edges and tons of snickerdoodle cookies lined up like little soldiers. But there were a lot of gaps in that formation. "Uh-huh." Ian was a surgeon. No way would he mess up that many times learning to use an egg flipper. She sent her uncle a knowing look. "How many have you broken so you could munch more?"

"Maybe a dozen," Uncle Warny confessed, his cheeks turning ruddy. "But that's for me and Jake together." He waved a finger between his chest and the dog.

"Of course." She ate a bite of cereal, which not only looked but also tasted like tree bark, and watched Ian lift the cookies from the cookie sheet to the wax paper. No problem whatsoever. "He's a pretty quick study."

"He's eager to please you." Uncle Warny's voice warmed and his eyes glossed. "He's a good man, Maggie girl."

"Yes, he is." She took another bite of her cereal, swallowed and bit her lips to hold off a smile. Never before had Uncle Warny given any man his stamp of approval. Not James Parker in tenth grade, not Donald Greer in college. He'd gotten a snort, which proved to be about what he should have gotten. But Ian and his devotion, his eagerness to please, had gotten approval. That warmed her heart.

The Christmas music stopped. Maggie stilled, instinctively reaching for her gun.

"It's okay." Ian stayed her hand. "Warny, you want to handle the CD?"

"CD?" He grunted and hauled himself to his feet. "My boy, these ain't no newfangled CDs. They're honest-to-goodness albums. Been around here for years and years." He lumbered toward the living room and yelled back, "Jake, don't you snitch that cookie."

Maggie whipped around and saw Jake snitch a cookie from the edge of the bar. "Oh, you are so busted."

Ian laughed. "Warny put it on the edge so Jake could get it."

Maggie wrinkled her nose, the tension draining from her body, and whispered, loving the twinkle in Ian's eyes, "I know."

They spent the rest of the morning baking cookies, decorating the tree, stringing lights along the front porch and draping the netted ones on the bushes, and wrapping the front porch columns. Swags of fresh-scented pine hung in low-slung ropes along the mantel with huge red bows on each end and dead center. The Nativity set was in its place atop the piano, and the photos had been bunched closer together to make plenty of room.

"Where's baby Jesus?" Ian asked, studying the aged set.

"He doesn't get into the manger until Christmas Eve, when he's born."

"My grandfather used to do that." Ian smiled.

Maggie's heart skipped a full beat. "I'm so glad you're enjoying remembering your traditions, too."

"I am, Maggie." He looked away, studied the tree.

"I missed them. Who wouldn't? But it just didn't seem right to celebrate—until this year."

Her breath hung in her throat. "Everything's different now, isn't it?"

"It is." He didn't seem troubled by that. "Can we put a twig of mistletoe right here?" He pointed to the light fixture in the ceiling just inside the entryway at the front door. "We always did that at home."

"Absolutely." She dragged the stepladder over and hung it. "Look okay?"

Ian held the ladder steady. "Looks great."

"Ian Crane, you didn't even look at it." She rocked the ladder and grabbed his shoulder to steady herself.

He cranked back his head. "I see you standing under it, which means you owe me a kiss, Maggie Mason."

She laughed. "Indeed I do." Bending, she claimed his lips.

Uncle Warny grunted. "Jake, my boy, I think we might just see mistletoe hanging all over the place this year." He let out a soft chuckle.

"Woof!"

"All right then." Warny lumbered back into the kitchen. "You flea-bitten hound. I told you not to snitch that cookie." His voice dropped. "Here you go, boy. Now this is absolutely the last one…"

"Got your weapon ready?"

Maggie nodded at Ian. Crawford had likely long since been gone, but one didn't assume anything about him twice. They stepped out the back door. "We still have to decorate the fir." Maggie glanced at the tree in question on the way to Ian's SUV.

"It's special to you?" Ian walked beside her.

She nodded. "And to Paul. Our mother had a perfect

tree. Every ornament and bow and bit of garland had to be hung just so. No self-respecting icicle dared to crimp out of place on her tree."

"Let me guess." He lifted a fingertip. "You and Paul weren't allowed to touch it."

"Touch it? She barely allowed us to breathe in the same room with it." Maggie grunted, cautiously scanning the woods, down toward the creek. "Uncle Warny brought Paul and me three big boxes of decorations and told us to decorate the fir. It could be our tree." She smiled at the fond memory. "So we decorated the fir our way."

"Your uncle is a special man."

"He knows what matters." She smiled. "Paul called while you were on the phone with Madison. The weather's finally broken. They can't get out yet, but with luck, they'll make it home by Christmas."

"That's great news." Ian brightened. "It can't be your best Christmas unless Paul's here."

Ian cared and he was trying so hard to make the holiday special for her. It wouldn't be the best Christmas without Paul, but it would be good. She wanted it to be special for Ian, too. "After the last few years we've both had, being here, together…it's going to be a great Christmas."

"It is, isn't it?" He looked away, and then said, "Maggie, would it be okay if we brought Beth some flowers after our shopping today? I mean, would that bother you?"

"Of course not." She automatically checked the vehicle for explosives with Ian.

"Clear."

"Clear." She climbed into the SUV.

"You're sure. I don't want you to feel—"

"I loved her, too, Ian. I'm sure."

He nodded, opened the driver's door. "She loved poinsettias."

"White ones, not red." Maggie recalled. "We'll shop and pick up one, then run it out to her. And afterward, I think we deserve a special treat." The decorations looked beautiful, the ranch smelled of cookies and home. Perfect...except for Crawford's interference.

Ian slid in beside her. "What kind of special treat?" He cranked the engine. It roared to life. "Wait. Let me guess. Whatever it is, it's at Miss Addie's Café, right?"

She nodded enthusiastically. "It's Friday. During the season, she has Christmas cakes every Friday."

"I hope one is carrot cake. I haven't had a good carrot cake in...a long time."

"Ooh, me, either." Maggie clasped his hand. "Beth made the best I've ever eaten. But don't tell Miss Addie. Her icing is really good—and she does bake them—but Beth's had something that isn't in Miss Addie's. I have no idea what it was, but it was delicious."

"It was her secret ingredient. Anytime anyone asked, she'd say, 'That's the love.'"

Maggie smiled. "It probably was."

"Definitely," Ian said, "and a dash of vanilla nut. But don't tell."

"Your secret is safe with me." She crossed her heart. "I'm surprised Beth told you."

"She didn't." He gave her a wonderful mischievous look. "I peeked."

Maggie laughed, lush and deep. "Shame on you."

"I'm awful, but I never told another soul."

"Ian Crane, you just told me."

"That's different."

"Why?"

"Because you're the other half..." He faltered. "It just is," he said, then quickly changed the subject. "You having carrot cake at Miss Addie's, too?"

She didn't dare make too much of it. His other half, he'd started to say, but he hadn't. He'd stopped himself, and she couldn't afford to forget that. Still, her heart could long to hear the rest of it. It could...even if it shouldn't. Even if longing for his love was absolutely the last thing she should do. Her head understood the logic in that perfectly. Her heart didn't. Either by choice or stubbornness, it felt what it felt, and while she wouldn't let herself think the word, apparently her heart had no reservation in feeling it. That had to be squelched...she supposed. Didn't it?

"Carrot cake?"

"Sorry, I drifted."

"I'll say. So...?"

"Nope, no carrot cake this time." Maggie rubbed her tummy. "Red velvet." She feigned a swoon. "Miss Addie's red velvet cake is simply the best anywhere in the country."

"Mmm, with an endorsement like that, it's going to be hard to resist."

"It's a tough call. Oh, but her key lime pie. Mmm, I love her key lime pie."

"Stop. You keep this up, and on the way back we'll have to stop at the weigh station like the trucks."

"It's hard, Ian." She fished in her purse for her sunglasses. The day had turned even drearier, but the glare was as bad as the sun. "I've missed...everything." She seated the glasses at the bridge of her nose. "I'm home and...I'm home."

He lifted their clasped hands to his lips and pecked a gentle kiss to her wrist. "So we're shopping, doing flowers and having cake—and maybe just a sliver of key lime pie." Ian grunted. "It's beginning to feel a lot like Christmas."

"It is." Maggie's throat went thick. "Thank you for that, Ian."

"Thank you for that, Maggie."

He squeezed her hand and drove to North Bay.

"Miss Addie!"

Ian hung back and watched Maggie wrap the frail Miss Addie in a bear hug. Gracie, her seven-year-old granddaughter, stood beside him, absorbed in the exchange.

The two women both talked at once, and every head in the place turned to see what had them in a ruckus.

Then Gracie saw her face. "Maggie!" She flew into her arms, jumped and wrapped her legs around Maggie's hips.

Maggie caught her, squealed and spun in a circle. "Oh, Gracie! You're so big." She squeezed her, and then eased her head back. "Let me see you."

Gracie lifted her precocious chin. "It's the same. Hardly changed at all."

"Oh, but it has, Gracie." Maggie studied her carefully. "Your cheekbones are higher and your skin—you've been eating your growing food. You're so beautiful."

"I'm not. I don't have all my teeth." She spread her lips, revealing a gap where a front tooth had been.

"The new one's on the way. Another month and you'll be stunning." Maggie's eyes softened. "You look so much like your mother."

"She ain't dead, Maggie."

Maggie knew she wasn't dead, but she didn't know

what Miss Addie had elected to tell her granddaughter about her mother. Maggie had found her six months ago in Atlanta, living between a shelter and the streets, strung out on drugs. She'd tried to get her into rehab, but the woman wanted no part of it. Knowing it wouldn't work without her cooperation, she'd called Miss Addie and given her the report on her daughter. Maggie cast a glance at Miss Addie. "That's good news, I'm sure."

"It's great news," Gracie confided. "Gran doesn't cry as much anymore. But we still pray for her every day."

"That's wonderful." Still, Miss Addie didn't send the first signal. Maggie wasn't sure what to say or do.

Ian appreciated her caution. He'd not been a parent but if he had, he'd like that kind of care exercised with his kids.

Maggie stroked Gracie's hair. "We don't have to talk about it if you'd rather not."

"I ain't talking about her at all except to tell you she ain't dead. Gran says that's the Christian thing to do, in case you're praying for the wrong thing."

"Ah, well, your Gran is very smart about these things, so we'll just listen to her on it."

Gracie twisted her mouth to say something, decided against it and nodded.

"So sit down, sit down." Miss Addie fluttered, her apron splattered with tiny wet spots. She'd clearly been in the kitchen all day.

Maggie put Gracie down and took a seat at the table. Ian sat across from her.

Miss Addie clasped his shoulder. "You're looking good, Ian. I'm glad to see it."

"Thank you." He smiled. She'd been nagging him for months to quit scowling and find something in his life to be joyful about. He hadn't done it. He'd tried but couldn't find his way until he'd watched Maggie. Then he realized that hiding behind the past and the hurt was being a coward, and Beth would hate that. So did he. That's a lot of what had his feelings so jumbled up about Maggie. It felt like love, but it could be the absence of nothing. When you're feeling nothing, and all of a sudden you're laughing and excited and even needing the company of a beautiful woman, and you're noticing so many wonderful things about her you hadn't noticed before…well, it confused him. He wasn't too proud to admit it. It felt like love. But was it?

Maggie was right. They did love each other. But it sure felt a lot like falling in love, too. Standing, holding that ladder, looking up at her hanging that mistletoe…

Heaven help him.

"Ian." Maggie leaned over and touched his hand. "The menu. Miss Addie's asking what we want."

He smiled. "Sorry, Miss Addie. We've been on a marathon shopping run. I'm dragging."

"From shopping?" Gracie looked stunned.

"Well, I baked cookies, then we decorated the tree and the house and everything else—"

"Except the fir," Maggie interjected.

"Except the fir," he conceded. "Then we went shopping."

"Oh, my." Miss Addie touched a hand to her face. "You're with one of the two shopping queens. Back in the day, when Maggie Mason and Madison McKay went shopping, every storekeeper in North Bay celebrated. Nobody can outlast those two shopping."

Didn't surprise Ian. "And I'm out of practice."

"So let's get you some hot coffee to warm your bones and…what kind of food?"

"Dessert." He lifted the menu.

"We're torn," Maggie said. "I've missed everything. Ian wants carrot cake, I want red velvet, but I really want key lime pie, too."

"Oh, hon. Wait. You remember the year you turned thirteen and I made you a queen cake?"

"What's a queen cake?" Gracie asked her gran.

Miss Addie's eyes twinkled. "When you turn twelve, I'll tell you. But—" she looked at Maggie "—it just so happens Adeline Cray was in with her Rebecca, and she turned thirteen today, so I baked one."

"Oh, I love it." Maggie bounced in her chair. "Now I have to pick one!"

Miss Addie sniffed. "Long as you been gone from home, girl, no, by gum, you don't. You leave it to me." She winked and then disappeared into the kitchen.

Gracie waited until Miss Addie couldn't see her. "Maggie, my mom's on drugs. That's why she stays away. I hate drugs, and I'm mad at her for it."

"Mad at her?" Ian asked.

"She loves them more than us."

"She doesn't—" Maggie started.

"Gracie," Ian interrupted. "You know I'm a doctor, right?"

She nodded.

"Your mom loves you. She's what we call an addict."

"Ian, I don't know if Miss Addie would approve—"

He ignored Maggie. "Her body has gotten used to the drugs, and now if it doesn't get them, she gets really, really sick."

"I didn't know she got sick."

"If she doesn't get the drugs into her body, she does. We could help her with that, if she'd let us, but that's a hard thing to do when you're sick. It doesn't mean she doesn't love you, honey. It means she's fighting a war inside her body, and right now she's losing."

"But she won't always lose, right?"

"I hope not." He clasped her shoulder. "The truth is, sometimes people win and sometimes drugs do. We just have to hope this time your mom does."

"I'll pray."

"That would be…" He stopped, thought it through. "Prayer is the best hope there is for your mom, Gracie."

"Dr. Crane?"

"Yes, Gracie?"

"Will you pray for my mom, too?"

Ian could feel Maggie's eyes boring through him, but his answer would be the same either way. "I will, Gracie."

She smiled. "You, too, Maggie?"

"Every day, sweetheart."

"Maybe with us all praying it'll work. Gran does, too. That's four of us. God can probably hear four of us."

"Well," Maggie said, propping her chin on her hand, her elbow on the table, "my uncle Warny says God hears every single prayer a child says. They're special to Him, and He always, always hears them."

Gracie thought about that. "He would know 'cause he's old. Old people know lots of stuff."

"He's always known a lot of stuff." Maggie nodded.

Miss Addie came out carrying two mugs of steaming-hot coffee and a platter. "Gracie, get Maggie and Ian some water, hon."

"Yes, ma'am." She started to move. "Oh, wait. Maggie, tomorrow night you and Dr. Crane have to come to our Christmas program at church. I'm gonna be Mary."

"You are?" Maggie asked. She'd been an angel for three years and wanted to be Mary so badly she couldn't see straight. Another important development Maggie had missed with this last move. "What time?"

"Six o'clock. You'll come, won't you?"

"You bet we'll be there, won't we, Ian?" Maggie looked at him with such hope. "Gracie being Mary is a huge, huge deal. She's worked hard for this for a long time."

"That is a very big deal." He gave her a solemn nod. "We wouldn't miss it, Gracie."

Smiling ear to ear, she fairly floated to get their water.

"Wonderful." Miss Addie set a tray down in the center of the table. "Another problem solved." She dropped her voice. "She's pretty peeved at her mother."

"Mmm."

"It means a lot to her that you'll be going to see her be Mary, Maggie."

"Wouldn't miss it, Miss Addie," Maggie repeated. "I know how long she's wanted this."

"That she has." She clicked her tongue to the roof of her mouth. "I fixed you two a sampler. Three little pieces of everything." She backed up. "You can both try everything and then fight over who gets the third piece of whatever." She laughed.

Maggie squealed and hugged Miss Addie. "I just love you."

"We love you, too, dear heart." Miss Addie sniffed. "About time you got yourself home." She gave Maggie a hard pat, and then backed away. "Now, eat yourselves sick."

To laughter and lighthearted banter, they tried.

He sat alone at a table just inside the door, listening and watching the exchange. She looked straight at him.

Slightly, he dipped his chin.

She visibly relaxed, nodded back, and then returned her attention to the kid.

Maggie wasn't a mother, but she had listened to the child and given her all of her attention. So had Ian Crane. And he'd been honest but compassionate in talking to the kid about her mother's drug addiction.

They weren't too busy. Otherwise occupied. Or present but not really there.

His stomach churned. He had to stop. He couldn't see them this way. Their concern for the kid couldn't be real. What did they care about her or her mother?

And Maggie sitting there throwing around *I love you* to that twig of a woman, Addie, as if it meant nothing. Those words were sacred. How dare she toss them out as if they were cheap junk?

His ears perked. So they'd be at the Christmas program tomorrow night, would they? The wheels in his mind started turning, spinning fast, then suddenly stopped. Well, so would he.

And come Christmas, news of what happened would be on every channel nonstop all day.

Merry Christmas, Maggie Mason.

With this slight revision in his plan, it was critical he get back to the ranch before they did. He dropped a few bills on the table and then eased out the door.

EIGHT

Maggie walked into the packed church beside Ian, who remained patient while she greeted people she hadn't seen in ages. Still, she didn't want to push it. He hadn't been inside the church since Beth had died, and he likely wouldn't be in it tonight if Gracie hadn't pulled his heartstrings.

She'd worried about him maybe changing his mind until he'd declared that there wasn't time to decorate the fir and get into town in time for the program. Only a blind woman would have missed the hint that he hoped decorating the fir was more important to her and they could skip the Christmas program, but Gracie would be so disappointed. They had to go, Maggie had insisted. The last thing that child needed was another adult breaking promises to her.

That had gotten Ian into a navy suit that did amazing things to his eyes and had an equally amazing effect on Maggie's heart rate.

She was in real trouble on that front, and she knew it. When or how she wasn't sure, but Ian Crane had her full attention, and it didn't seem likely that all the rational reasons in the world for keeping her distance because of Crawford were going to do a thing to convince her heart to shield itself. *It is what it is, and things are what they are.*

Ian led her to seats near Miss Addie. "The decorations look really pretty, don't you think?" he said.

"Gorgeous." Maggie felt almost giddy. At home for Christmas, in her own church's gathering room, with her own friends and Ian. She looked at the Christmas tree, listened to the adult choir sing "Joy to the World" and then "It Came Upon a Midnight Clear." They continued singing songs while people filled the seats. Maggie looked at the children, the happy and expectant faces of both them and their parents, and saw a family with three children, one of whom was an infant. They looked adorable, all dressed in green. A little sigh escaped her. A family. Her heart hitched. One day... For now she didn't dare to dream. The agony of Crawford coming after her was horrific. But imagine if he were after her child. Her heart couldn't bear it. Yet tonight she wasn't running, or alone in a strange house indulging in her annual Ben & Jerry's ice cream and hot bubble bath pity party because she was isolated. Tonight she was home with people who knew and loved her, and they were celebrating Christmas. She and Ian, in church together, celebrating Christmas. Peace and contentment filled her. Sometimes life was just so good.

"Maggie! Maggie!" Gracie ran up to her, her head covered in a long white cotton scarf and her robe covering all but the tips of her toes. "You came!"

"Ian and I told you we would."

Gracie gave her a gap-toothed smile. "But you really did it."

Relief that she hadn't given in to temptation and stayed home to decorate the fir had her knees weak. "Of course." Gracie's arm was bent. She held something behind her back. "What are you hiding?" Something for her gran, probably.

She smiled and whipped out a black rose. "It's for you."

Maggie went on full alert. So did Ian.

"Where did you get that, Gracie?" Ian asked before Maggie could.

"The man gave it to me. He said to give it to you and to tell you that you look pretty in red."

Crawford was here! "What did he look like?"

Gracie described him. Shorter and heavier than Ian, brown hair, tanned, wearing a black suit and a red tie.

She looked at Ian. "I saw Detective Cray and his wife three rows up, center aisle from the door. Clear the church." Maggie touched Addie's shoulder, interrupting her conversation with Liz Palmer, sitting on her right. "We have to get everyone out of here. Quickly."

Addie's gaze collided with Maggie's and she nodded, answering the unspoken question. She gained her feet. "Liz, start evacuating—right now. Orderly, so we don't scare the kids."

"Gracie, go with your gran."

"But I have to get back—"

"Go with your gran right now."

She frowned but went, and Maggie headed for the front of the stage, grabbed the mike and forced a calm into her voice she didn't feel. "Attention. Attention, everyone."

The low rumble quieted and a hush fell over those gathered.

"A situation has arisen and we need to vacate the premises immediately. Please don't linger, just use the nearest exit to you and walk outside and wait across the street until the authorities—"

The pastor came running up to her. "Maggie, what are you doing?"

"—clear the premises and tell us we can return. Go now, please. Hurry, but be safe and orderly…just like in the fire drills at school."

"Maggie Mason, if this is a prank…"

She covered the mike with her hand and shot the pastor a hard look. "The serial killer who loves bombs and is trying to kill me is here. We have to vacate the building to make sure no one gets hurt."

His mouth dropped in a big O.

Ian and Detective Cray, several people she recognized as volunteers with the fire department, and General Talbot and Colonel Dayton ushered people out the doors.

Maggie started searching, automatically calling Ian on her cell. When he answered, she asked, "Did you call Beecher?"

"He's here. His equipment is not. The team is on the way with it."

"Get them across the street, Ian." She couldn't see him and could barely hear him over the din of raised voices and screaming kids. "Keep people out of their cars and away from the parking lot. It'd be just like Crawford—"

A huge explosion rocked the walls, set her ears to ringing.

"Maggie! Maggie!"

She dropped to a crouch, looked around. "It's not in here. I'm fine."

"The parking lot's on fire!" a man yelled.

A series of secondary explosions ripped through the air. Screams flooded the gathering room, carried inside from outside the church.

"He got the cars," she told Ian. "That's just one round. There's a second one somewhere—I'm betting in here." The gathering room had cleared. She started scanning, looking for a device.

"Get out of there, Maggie."

"He always works in twos. Always, Ian. There's a second bomb somewhere."

"You can't find it if you're dead. Evacuate now."

He was running, trying to get to her. Her heart sank. "Don't come in. Please don't. I love you, Ian. I can't live with knowing I'm the reason you're…"

"Leave it to Beecher to find. Do you hear me, Maggie?" Panicked. Terrified.

Nothing along the edge of the stage. Nothing in or under the piano. Nothing wired into the potted plants decorating the stage, or in the festive tree strung with popcorn and handmade ornaments. "It's here. I know it's here."

She dropped to the floor, lay flat on her stomach. "I have to go. I need the flashlight app on my phone." She hung up. Punched the screen to pull up the app and flooded the underside of the rows of chairs with light.

Nothing.

She stepped onto the stage. Examined the life-size crèche. Checked the statues of the animals. The manger. She reached for a handful of hay and saw the device. Called Ian. "I found it. It's in the manger." Bold red numerals flashed. "Beecher's got three minutes and twelve seconds."

"He's on the way."

"Anyone hurt?"

"No. No, but, Maggie, will you please get out of there?"

"When Beecher gets here. I have to make sure no one else comes in."

"But, Maggie—"

"He's here." She hung up. "Beecher, up here!"

He ran over to her, followed by the same two team members who had been at the ranch. One was Thompson. She didn't know the name of the other one.

Beecher scanned the device. "This one is hot. Go outside, Maggie."

"Can you disarm it?"

"Yes." He spared her a glance. "Go! You're slowing us down."

Maggie ran out of the building and into a plume of black smoke. Two cars in the parking lot had exploded. She found Ian. "You're sure no one was hurt?"

"I'm sure." He looked over at her. "What's going on inside?"

"Beecher said he could disarm it. I saw plastics. Probably enough C-4 to take down the building."

"That's what Crawford wanted."

She frowned, her jaw trembling. "Yes."

Ian wrapped an arm around her shoulder. "We're fine. They're all fine. No one was hurt."

"He wanted to kill as many of us as he could, Ian."

"But he didn't."

"But he wanted to, and he could try again."

"Yes, he could. And if he does, we'll deal with it. Right now, let's get everyone farther away from the building."

"Miss Addie's Café's parking lot," Maggie suggested. "Upwind from the smoke."

"Let's move."

People moved surprisingly fast. They were loud, nervous, wary, but working to calm down the children and account for everyone.

The fire department put out the fire on the cars, and the smoke started clearing. Finally, Beecher surfaced with his team and they evacuated the device on a tank-looking truck that had a police escort. Maggie nudged Ian to look. "Where will they take it?"

"Probably to the base." He noticed her shaking and wrapped an arm around her shoulder. "It's all going to be okay, Maggie."

"I ruined the play for the children."

"No, you didn't. Crawford did." Ian dropped his voice. "Gracie said that the man left in a black car. She watched him drive away before she came inside. So he's not here anymore."

How had Ian known she feared Crawford had stood beside her and she hadn't known it? When had he learned to read her so well? "We need to get details from Gracie right away."

"As soon as the police are done."

"We know," Ian said, "that Blue Shoes isn't Talbot or Dayton."

"We do?" It was Crawford. It had to be Crawford.

"Gracie would have known either of them. They're in Miss Addie's all the time. She didn't know the man who gave her the rose."

They were, and she didn't. Unfortunately, the description of the man she'd shared didn't fit them or Crawford. Had to be a disguise. And his blue shoes had been spotted out behind the ranch several times. Paul had chased him on a horse, but Blue Shoes escaped on a four-wheeler. They couldn't be dealing with an unknown.

Pastor Brown found her. "I'm sorry, Maggie. I should

have listened immediately without questioning you."
His balding pate caught the light from a streetlamp and
reflected a sheen. "The children could have…"

"They're fine, Pastor. We're all fine."

"But, Gran, baby Jesus isn't in the manger," Gracie
told Miss Addie. "We can't do this another time. Tomorrow's Christmas Eve."

The children were all upset that the program had
been ruined. Guilt swamped Maggie.

Pastor Brown heard Gracie and turned. "Ian, has the
church been cleared?"

"The gathering room has, but not the rest of the
building."

"Come with me." He motioned for Ian to follow.

"Where are you going?" Maggie asked.

"To get the crèche and manger and the rest of the
Nativity. We're going to have this program right here
in Miss Addie's parking lot."

The children squealed their delight.

A few other men took off after Ian and the pastor,
and they soon formed a line that shifted folded chairs
into the parking lot. In less than thirty minutes, even
the decorated tree was in place—everything but the
stage, which didn't seem to bother the children a bit.

Their tears stopped.

Their long faces turned to smiles.

And their Christmas program was now about to
begin.

"I should go," Maggie told Miss Addie. "Tell Gracie I'm sorry she didn't get to be Mary on the stage."

"Go where?"

"This whole mess of their program is my fault. I
should leave so they can enjoy it."

"Absolutely not." Miss Addie took on the same tone

she used to scold Gracie. "You park yourself in that seat right there, Maggie Mason."

"But—"

"But nothing. We're people of faith, girl. We stand together. You leave now, what kind of example are you setting for the children? That when one of us is in trouble, we all turn tail and run, or shun our own? Is that what you want them to think?"

"Of course not." Maggie gasped. "But he could come back."

"If he does, we'll know it," Liz said. "Gracie got a good look at him and we're spreading the word. We're watching for him now."

"You're sure, Miss Addie?"

"Absolutely certain." She patted the seat next to hers.

Maggie looked at Ian.

"I agree with them," he said.

Maggie smiled, sat down and soon the program began. One of the three kings lost his turban. A shepherd tripped over a cow and kissed the concrete, but he jumped up and warned his mom with a raised hand to stay away, he was fine. Maggie watched them reenact the Christmas story with wonder and delight. When the piano would have been played, all the audience hummed and the children sang.

Ian looked at her and smiled. "You're bemused."

"Totally," Maggie whispered and watched Gracie, her little face so serious, her voice so earnest, carry across the hushed crowd. Ever so gently she put the baby Jesus in the manger. Her reverence and care humbled Maggie. "Gracie's just the best Mary ever," she whispered softly to Miss Addie.

"She's worn out a doll practicing."

Maggie smiled and watched.

Ian clasped her hand. "Thank you, Maggie."

She looked over at him. "For what?"

"Making me come tonight." His warm breath fanned her face. "I'd forgotten how terrific these people are. Now I remember."

Ian had reclaimed his church family.

A lump rose in Maggie's throat and she smiled. Crawford intended to cause tragedy. Instead the opposite had happened. His twisted cruelty had brought their community closer, and because it had, the children wouldn't be leaving church tonight traumatized but all aflutter at their special Christmas program held in Miss Addie's Café's parking lot.

God promised that what others intended for harm, He'd turn to good, and He had.

"Talbot and Dayton—"

"It's not them. It's Gary Crawford, Ian. Gracie's description is generic, but not one thing points to anyone else." The only question in her mind was if Crawford killed David Pace and maybe even Beth.

Oh, but she hoped he hadn't. Ian could forgive Maggie many things, but the serial killer after her killing his wife simply because she was Maggie's check-in buddy? That would be too much for anyone to forget, much less accept or forgive.

A pang of regret threatened the spark of hope in her heart that somehow a way would appear for a future with Ian. She couldn't see a way, not so long as Crawford was alive, but if he'd killed Beth, then even his death wouldn't set Maggie free, and it sure wouldn't endear her to Ian. He'd hate her forever—and she couldn't blame him.

Any hopes for more between them seemed doomed and foolish. She stiffened. From the start, she'd known they would be, and she'd warned herself over and again not to fall in love with him. Not to ruin a perfectly good friendship—a special friendship—that if lost would leave her wanting and mourning.

But her heart hadn't listened. And now with Talbot and Dayton cleared…it looked more and more as if Crawford had staged all the challenges in North Bay. Well, except those actually caused by Della's ex.

And because the possibility of Crawford's guilt rang true deep down inside and stood up to the test of her skilled instincts, to Maggie, the magical night suddenly seemed dimmer. Dimmer and sadder and lonelier, though she sat surrounded by people she knew and cared about and some she loved.

And that truth left her wondering.

Where would Crawford strike her next?

"It's after five, Maggie girl." Uncle Warny fussed with his tie. "You ain't planning on going to the Christmas Eve service?"

She sat at the kitchen table, her chin braced with her hand atop the table. "No, I'm not going."

"Why not? You always loved the Christmas candlelight service. You ain't sick—"

"I'm fine." She staved off a sigh. "I think I've caused enough excitement at church already. They should have a peaceful service on Christmas Eve."

"Ah, I see." Uncle Warny let go of the tie, which was decidedly crooked, and sat down. "Fix this thing before I choke myself to death, will you?"

Maggie stood up, tried adjusting his tie, gave up and started over.

"I figure you ain't meaning to snub the folks here,

though by hiding out at home that's exactly what you're doing, sweet pea."

"I'm not a coward." She glared at him. "I'm trying to not get them killed."

"Nobody got hurt last night."

"If Luke Sampson had gone back to his car for Elizabeth's sweater a minute sooner, she'd be a widow this morning." Maggie's stomach soured, tensed. They had two little ones at home.

"Luke's fine. Elizabeth's fine. Their kids are fine. Everybody's fine." He looked deeply into her eyes, hesitated for a long moment, then said, "Maggie, I admire what you been doing, trying to keep Paul and me safe, but that Crawford is right about one thing. You can't hide. And, to my way of thinking, you can't run anymore, either."

"What do you suggest I do, then?" She pulled the tie sharply, smoothed it down and then returned to her chair and plopped down. "I don't have a lot of options."

"I suggest you pray."

She looked over at him. "I do, Uncle Warny. All the time. Mostly that he doesn't murder anyone else. And that I get to live another day."

"I say put on your Sunday finest then, and let's go hunting."

He wanted her to hunt down Crawford. "I have hunted him. And hunted him and hunted him." She shuddered. "He could be anyone."

"Maybe you're right." He stood up. "Maybe it's best you stay put here until we know his face." He gave Jake a dog biscuit, then paused and looked back at Maggie. "Ian's a good man, Maggie girl. I hope you don't get no foolish ideas about protecting him by shutting him out of your life." He rubbed at his neck. "That'd surely hurt him in the heart, and I believe it's been home to enough pain already. Just something to think about."

She wanted to rebel. How painful would it be if he learned Beth was dead and it was Maggie's fault?

But she didn't. She sat silently and watched her uncle leave for church.

She should go decorate the fir. She should, but Ian was napping and doing it alone…her heart wasn't in it.

The phone rang.

She checked caller ID. It was Paul. She punched the button. "Hey, big brother." Surely he had to almost be home. They'd been reporting progress, and they couldn't be that far away.

The static in the phone was awful. She could barely hear him. "We're… Better tell Warny to shut up the barn… A bad storm…blowing through."

She made a mental note to check the weather report to find out the specifics of his warning. "I'm catching most of what you're saying, but not all of it," she told him. "I'll check the weather. When will you get here?"

"After… Storm is dropping slush and it's freezing up. Roads are deadly."

Disappointment bit her hard. He wouldn't make it home for Christmas. "Maybe you'd better find someplace safe to wait it out until the storm passes, Paul. It's not worth it."

"Let you know…when…stop."

"I think you said you'd let us know when you stopped. Call if you can. Just be careful. People down here have no idea how to drive on icy roads." There'd be a string of wrecks a mile long before morning.

The line went dead.

She hung up and turned, saw Ian standing in the

doorway, soaking wet. Definitely not sleeping. "What happened to you?"

"I locked down the barn and took care of the animals. A bad storm is coming."

"From the looks of you, it's already here." She grabbed a towel and brought it to him. "I'll snag something of Paul's for you to wear while your clothes are drying."

"Thanks."

She ran up to Paul's room for jeans and a shirt, and then returned to the kitchen with them.

He shot her an apologetic look. "Sorry about the fir."

"What about it?"

"We didn't get it decorated."

"It's okay." Not much about this Christmas at home was turning out as it had played in her mind. But that didn't mean it was awful. A lot of good had come from what had happened. It was just the possibility of Crawford and Beth weighing heavily on her mind. If nothing else, in these past three years of running, she'd learned to be flexible and adapt without drama. She'd had no choice and no one around to notice. Not much sense in engaging in drama when you're alone. God saw it all, of course. But He wasn't impressed with self-pity or with displays of drama. So she'd just stopped that— and wondered what merit Madison and she had seen in it as teens.

Ian lifted his arms, one higher than the other, then shifted them. "Monopoly or popcorn and a movie?"

Maybe the movie would do her good. Get her mind off herself and her troubles. "Movie." She smiled. "A Christmas one."

"Let me guess." Ian rubbed his chin, feigning deep consideration. *"It's a Wonderful Life."*

Her jaw dropped. "How did you know that?"

He smiled and his eyes twinkled. "You've watched it every year since you were in third grade, Maggie. It doesn't take Christmas magic to know…"

She stilled. "Do you remember everything I tell you?"

"Don't you?"

Her face heated. "I don't know. But can we not test it tonight?"

He swung an arm around her. "No tests. Just a quiet, no-stress evening eating popcorn and watching a movie."

A sigh of relief shuddered her shoulder. "Wonderful."

"Somebody's at the gate." Maggie heard the alarm.

Ian was already out of his seat and headed toward the monitor room. When Maggie stepped in, he told her, "It's Detective Cray."

"Buzz him in."

Ian stretched, tapped the buzzer and on the monitor Maggie watched the gate swing open. He drove through then up to the house, using the back door as everyone did.

She passed him a towel on the back porch. "Boy, it's really coming down out here."

"Worse, the roads are freezing up." Cray swiped at his face with the towel. "Thanks."

"Why are you all the way out here? Have the wrecks started already?"

"Not yet, but we're on alert for them." He blotted his face and took off his coat, then hung it on a peg out on the back porch. "Dripping. Sorry about that."

"Don't worry about it, Detective." Maggie urged him inside. "Come on in. It's cold out here."

His hands were red and raw from the damp cold. "If you run warm water over your hands you'll feel better quick. I'll get you a cup of coffee."

He moved to the sink. "Is it decaf? I've had a potful already tonight."

"It's decaf." Ian filled a mug and set it at the table. "Sit down."

Maggie sat across from him, between the two men. Ian was as perplexed as she, gauging by his pensive expression. "So what's wrong?"

He hesitated as if torn. As if he intended to share something but had second thoughts about it now that he was here.

"Detective?" Maggie tilted her head. "Are you okay?"

"No, Maggie, I'm not. I'm in a dilemma. I shouldn't be here. I shouldn't tell anyone what I'm about to tell you. But if I don't and something happens...I won't forgive myself. Ever."

Ian stiffened. "If it can cause harm, you've got to share it."

Maggie interceded. "It's not always that easy, Ian. Not when the news is official." She looked at Cray. "You're here about something official, but you're here personally, off the record and the clock."

"Yeah." Some of the tension fell from his face.

"Okay. So as a person, you've discovered something that could be problematic for us. For me. That means Crawford."

"Yeah."

He hadn't found him. He hadn't identified him. She'd have gotten that information through the agency. So it had to be local—the reporter. Where was that investigation? "You got new information on David Pace."

He didn't answer.

"Is that a yes, or a no?" Ian asked Cray.

"It's a yes," Maggie told Ian, then swiveled her gaze back to Cray. "Did you get the final report back from the Coroner?"

Again, no answer. Cray sat still as a stone statue.

"That's a yes," Ian said, clearly seeking confirmation.

Maggie switched hats. "Detective, confidentially I'm notifying you that I'm still an active agent with the FBI. I've been undercover, and staying undercover is crucial to my survival. Confidentially, I'm telling you I have reason to believe there's a connection between the murders of David Pace and Beth Crane. Confidentially, I'm telling you that whatever information you have in your professional capacity that you withhold could impede my investigation. You see—" she braced "—I believe Gary Crawford killed David Pace."

"Crawford killed Pace?" Cray asked, a little confused. "Why do you think so?"

"I can't prove it but Crawford is extremely clever, warped and vengeful. He'd be thrilled to see the general or the colonel blamed for murder. Setting up two upstanding, respected officers and watching them fall from grace. He'd love that—"

Cray interrupted. "And you're undercover?"

"Yes," she said. "I'm counting on your total discretion so you don't get me killed."

"I understand." He nodded slowly, still absorbing. "If you're active, then I have no ethical conflicts sharing information."

"No, you don't." Precisely why she'd told him. If in an ethical dilemma, whatever information he had must be important. "So what did you risk treacherous roads getting here to tell us?"

"A couple hours ago, I got a message to call the coroner. Not his usual telephone call. He sent his grandson to my house to summon me."

"Very odd."

"He didn't want me to come to his office. He asked me to come to his house." Cray frowned. "So I went."

"And?" Maggie asked.

"He said he'd been visited by Daniel L. Ford from Homeland Security. Ford told the coroner what to say and insisted he forge the David Pace report—it was a matter of national security."

Maggie's mind tumbled and reeled, mixing this in with all she knew about Crawford, his patterns, his history, his methods.

"Did the coroner do it?" Ian asked.

Cray nodded. "But he wanted me to know the truth... in case there was a connection."

"To what?" Ian asked.

"My death, Ian," Maggie said. The puzzle pieces slammed into place. He hadn't tracked her through her FBI connections but her military connections. Crawford hadn't stopped coming after her because he feared her profiling skills or because she was a loose end. He kept coming after her because he feared Beth had told him about her investigation of the Nest. That fit. "Homeland Security, you said?"

Cray nodded.

It did fit, but maybe she'd been wrong. This sounded more like Talbot or Dayton. "Did the coroner say what really happened to Pace?"

"He wasn't shot." Cray sipped at his steaming coffee. "There wasn't a mark on him, and the blue shoes didn't fit him, either. Too big. Pace had an embolism."

"A blood clot?" Ian sounded skeptical. "Then why the explosion? Why burn his car and make sure he's not burned? Why move the car and Pace's body to stage a crime? This makes no sense."

Maggie chewed on her lower lip. "Unfortunately it makes perfect sense." She risked a glance at Ian. "The embolism didn't just happen. It was inflicted."

"It was." Cray nodded. "The coroner was stumped at first. No fat from the marrow of a broken bone. No tumor."

"Only one thing left, then," Ian said. "Air bubbles."

"That's what the coroner thought. But Pace had no history of deep vein thrombosis and no needle marks in the usual places."

Maggie frowned. "Did he check between Pace's toes?" If his shoes were off and replaced with the neon blue ones, between the toes was a likely place.

"He did," Cray said. "Nothing."

Ian sighed. "What about the roof of his mouth? Or under his tongue."

Cray set down his cup, looked at Ian. "How'd you know that? Pace wasn't a druggie. Medical school, military or what?"

"Military." Ian held Cray's gaze. "It's a tactic we saw a lot in the Middle East."

"Well, it was used here." Cray looked from Maggie to Ian. "Under his tongue."

"So Pace was murdered with air," Maggie said. "And Homeland Security—" She stopped midsentence.

"What?" Ian asked her.

Maggie gripped the ledge of the table. "Did you

say the Homeland Security agent was named Daniel L. Ford?"

Cray nodded. "Yeah."

Shock pumped through her body. "He was Crawford."

"What?"

"Shh, wait," Ian told Cray. "Why is he Crawford, Maggie?"

"His mother. Her maiden name was Ford. And her first name was—"

"Danielle," Ian finished for her. "Does the coroner have a surveillance photo of him?"

Cray pulled a photo out of his shirt pocket. "This is him. I came hoping maybe one or the other of you would recognize him from your previous careers. I had a gut feeling something was wrong."

He had no idea how much. Maggie looked at the photo and into the face of the man trying to kill her. So many emotions rocketed through her body, if not seated, she would have staggered. He was an ordinary-looking man. Not handsome, not ugly, not strong and formidable-looking. He didn't look like any of the powerful, brilliant, elusive things she knew him to be or at all like his mother. He looked like a quiet, gentle man who lived down the block maybe, or— "Oh, Ian. He was at Miss Addie's. I saw him when we were there for dessert."

"He fits Gracie's description. But if he was at Miss Addie's, wouldn't Gracie have remembered him from there?"

"She's a child. Maybe or maybe not. You know how unreliable even adult eyewitnesses are."

"Wait. Are you saying this is Gary Crawford?" Cray asked.

"Yes." Ian studied the photo. "And apparently, he's also Mr. Blue Shoes." He shot a look at Cray. "He did put the blue shoes on Pace."

"Somebody did, posthumously."

"So nothing that's happened was Talbot or Dayton," Ian said. "It was all Gary Crawford."

"Looks that way to me." Cray grunted. "Hard to believe someone who looks so normal is so twisted, isn't it?"

"It always is," Maggie confessed, screwing up her courage to say the one thing she wished with every fiber of her being she didn't have to say. "Ian, you know that if Crawford is Blue Shoes and he did all he's done, then it's highly possible he was also responsible for Beth's murder."

Ian's gaze collided with Maggie's. Pain flashed through his eyes. "That's pretty much a given, Maggie. Beth was your check-in buddy. Your one daily contact. He went after her to isolate you."

Her throat swelled and regret flooded her. Regret and guilt. "I'm so sorry, Ian. If I could—"

"No." Ian reached across the table and snagged her hand, squeezed it hard. "No, you didn't do this."

"But if it hadn't been for me, Beth—"

"Maggie, don't. This is Crawford's fault. He killed Beth. He killed Pace. And if given half a chance, he'll kill you. Put the blame where it belongs. On his shoulders. Not yours."

"You can forgive me?" she asked. He couldn't. How could he?

"You haven't done anything, and Beth would be the first to say it."

Relief washed over Maggie. Relief and sorrow. "I'm

sorry anyway, and I was so afraid you'd never be able to forgive me…"

"Don't be." Ian gently squeezed her hand a second time. "I don't blame you, Maggie."

The urge to cry nearly brought her to her knees. She fought it with everything in her. If she cried now she'd never stop. She'd fall apart at the seams and Crawford would win.

Jake sprung from his bed to his feet. A low, throaty growl rattling in his throat.

"What's the matter, boy?" Ian stood up. "Maggie, check on Warny."

She grabbed the phone. He'd insisted on staying in his apartment in the barn with the animals in case they were uneasy about the storm. "The line's dead."

"Use your cell."

"Here, use mine." Cray passed her his phone.

She dialed the barn. It rang and rang. "No answer."

Jake still stood on alert, still growled and bared his teeth.

Ian rounded the edge of the table and checked the security monitors. "Maggie, when did Warny decorate the fir?"

"He didn't." Her mouth went dry. "He was at church."

"Somebody did."

Her gaze collided with Detective Cray's. "Crawford."

She headed to the monitor room.

The fir was alight and beautifully decorated with ornaments and tinsel blowing in the wind. Even through the rain, it looked gorgeous. And beneath it lay dozens of packages, all wrapped in shiny paper. Green, red, blue and gold and silver.

Cold chills swept up Maggie's spine, firing every nerve ending in her body at once.

"What are all those packages under it?" Cray asked.

Her voice came out stilted, stiff. "From the wires sticking out of the boxes, I'd say bombs."

"Definitely Crawford," Cray said.

Maggie agreed.

As they watched the twinkling lights, the tree exploded.

NINE

Jake barked, fierce enough to split eardrums, batted at the door and it opened. He took off out of it like a shot.

"Jake!" Maggie shouted at him. "Come back here!"

But Jake was giving chase. And he did not come back.

Maggie grabbed her coat. Ian stopped her. "Oh, no. You're not going out there. Not now."

Cray was on the phone, summoning reinforcements.

Maggie tried to pull free of Ian. "But Jake…"

"Maggie, you can't." Ian met and held her gaze. "Have faith."

"I'm glad you're back in touch with God, but He does help those who help themselves."

"Just stay put until backup arrives. Please." Ian grabbed her by the shoulders. "I can't lose you, too. Okay? I…can't." The struggle in him settled. "You need to notify the task force."

He was right.

Fifteen minutes later, a rain-drenched Jake appeared at the back door.

And in his mouth he carried a neon blue shoe.

"Wearing one shoe, he's still here." Ian moved Maggie away from the back door.

Her cell rang. She grabbed it off the kitchen counter and connected the call. "Mason."

"Merry Christmas, Maggie."

Crawford. "Why did you blow up my fir?"

"Because you loved it. Decorated it every year, I hear."

No emotion. Maybe for the same reason as Beth. To isolate Maggie from all she loved. She factored that into his psychological profile. Rushing sounds snagged her attention. Running through crackling leaves. He was still on the ranch or in the woods adjacent to it where he'd been glimpsed several times. "You lost a shoe. Must be uncomfortable—cold feet on the bare ground. Lots of twigs out there."

"You should be thanking me, not worrying about twigs or my feet. I took your fir, but I let your mutt live."

He had. Why hadn't he shot Jake? "I'd thank you if you'd stop killing and leave me alone. Why can't you do that?"

He cackled. "Scorpions sting because they're scorpions. The world made me what I am, Maggie. You should know that by now."

"If you believe that, then you're wrong." Agitated, she paced the kitchen. "You choose who you want to be. We all do." No more crunching. He couldn't be in the woods. He had to be on the ranch itself. If he were on the road, there'd be street sounds and there weren't any.

"My mother—"

"Was no worse than mine," she interrupted. "You were ignored because she was working all the time. She neglected you. Didn't attend all your events at school, make your lunches and all that. Well, guess what? Neither did mine. And unlike you, my father was here, too, and he didn't do any of those things, either. You use your mother as an excuse to kill and trash people's lives. But it's just an excuse to do what you want to do."

"You know nothing about my life."

"I know a good bit about your life, Daniel," she said, disclosing that his identity was no longer a secret. The officers in charge of his mother's murder had made notes on her young son. "You were small for your age. You got teased and beaten up. You blamed her for that, too. And—"

"Blamed her? I saved her!"

Hence the roses. His way of mourning his loss, but serving the greater good by setting the woman free. Classic, but no. No, his patterns weren't wholly consistent. "You killed her to put her out of her misery—or so you say. But that's not the truth. You killed her because you blamed her for your misery. You blamed her for all that happened to you."

Bells sounded in the distance. Church bells. He was on her homesite! The place on the ranch where, when all this started, she'd been about to build her home.

"Don't you dare judge me. Don't you dare."

Maggie shook all over. This could be the wisest choice or the dumbest move she'd ever made. But a knowing settled inside her. She had to follow it. "You can run. You cannot hide." She punched the screen to disconnect the call.

Ian and Cray looked at her as if she'd lost her mind.

"I know where he is." She grabbed her coat, slung it on.

"Down by the creek." Ian grabbed his coat, shoved his arm into his sleeve. "Where I caught a flash of him before on the ATV."

Maggie didn't answer. She couldn't. Ian would put himself in harm's way. Cray, too. She had to protect them. Crawford wouldn't stop. He'd never stop. He'd tag them loose ends and kill them, too.

"Cray and I will go," Ian said. "You check on Warny. He's still not answering his phone."

The barn was closer to her homesite, and it would keep Cray and Ian a safe distance away. "Be careful."

Once again, she would face Gary Crawford alone.

Maggie dipped her chin against the driving rain, torn between going to the barn to see about her uncle and getting to the homesite before Crawford got too far away to track.

If Uncle Warny were harmed, she wouldn't be able to leave him, and she would lose the chance to stop Crawford from killing again. Warny would tell her to go after Crawford.

Trying to move as quietly as possible—even the rain didn't drown out the sounds of snapping twigs under her feet—she made her way to the edge of the homesite and paused at a magnolia, using its wide trunk as cover. Scanning, she spotted him, limping from the site toward the woods.

She reached under her coat and pulled her gun from its holster at her waist. Her hands shook. She shook all over. Rushing her steps, she intercepted him. "Crawford! Stop right there." Hunching low to the ground, she prepared in case he turned and fired.

Only one hand was visible, and it was empty, but what caught her attention were his feet: one bare foot and one blue shoe.

Thank you, Jake.

Rising up, she moved in, began shouting through the rain, reading him his rights.

* * *

"Something's not right," Ian told Cray. "There's no sign of anyone down here."

"She was wrong." Cray shielded his eyes from the icy rain to look at Ian. "We better get to the barn and see about her and Warny."

"She's not at the barn." Ian's jaw went stiff. He'd assumed Crawford was at the creek because he'd glimpsed him there before. She hadn't lied. Just let him assume. Fear rippled through his body. "She's protecting us. She knows where he is, and it's not at the barn." Where would Crawford go?

"Where then?"

"Somewhere that means something to her. He blew up her tree because she loved it, right? He'd be somewhere that matters."

"Something signaled her where he was."

Had to be sound. Sound...the church bells. "Her homesite."

"What homesite?"

"The site Maggie had cleared to build a home before Crawford started up." Ian moved. "Let's go."

"Surely the woman isn't confronting him on her own. Surely— That's exactly what she's doing, isn't it? She stayed away to protect her family. Now she's protecting you."

"And you. And if she's still alive, I'm going to make her wish she wasn't for doing it, too." Ian rushed his steps. "Oh, please, God, let her still be alive."

Maggie tripped over a stump and nearly went down.

A second was all Crawford needed. He whipped out a weapon, drew down on her. "Well, now we have a little dilemma. You have a gun. I have a gun. Who'll shoot first?"

On her stomach on the cold ground, she kept a two-handed aim on him. If she tried to get up, he'd shoot. She had no choice but to stay put. "I thought you'd be taller."

"What?" He chuckled. "Never mind. I thought you'd be smarter. It's been difficult to lead you every step of the way, Maggie."

"Not every step. For a while, I thought so, but that's just not true. I held my own against you just fine."

"A little credit is due, but you are, after all, the one on your belly in the dirt."

He had a point. "Why did you kill Beth and David Pace?"

He paused a long second and then shrugged, rain pelting his black trench coat. "Scorpions do what scorpions do."

"Glib, but not the truth. It wasn't related to me." The truth hit her. "It was because of your Homeland Security work." He couldn't afford for his connection there to be exposed. That's how he'd tracked her. Through those connections.

"Was it, now?"

It had to be. "I thought it was because Beth and I were check-in buddies, but it wasn't. It was about the Nest and keeping your affiliation to it secret."

"Tsk-tsk. You're not supposed to talk about that place." He grunted. "So little respect for rules, Maggie. I'm shocked."

"You know all about the Nest. You've been there— actually, you've seen parts of it that I haven't. And you're going to shoot me." She tried to lull him into complacency. "I want to know the truth. Are you even capable of telling the truth anymore?"

"Maybe they asked questions I didn't want to answer. It could be just that simple." He laughed. "You're not surprised that I know all about the Nest. Interesting. It is an enormously huge project, of course. Anytime you get that many people involved, it's impossible to prevent leaks." He stepped closer to her. "People just aren't as concerned as they once were with personal integrity or honor, are they? Hugely disappointing, that."

He was definitely out of his mind. "You routed your calls to me through the installation there. Which means you had access."

He feigned a sigh. "You're boring me now, Maggie."

"Ah, yes. The urge to kill again has been building hasn't it? You're almost out of time. You're deep into your two weeks."

"Well, at least you picked up on that pattern. You've missed quite a few."

Maybe she had. She didn't think so, but maybe she had. "Why do you do it?"

He glared at her, rain sliding in sheets down his face. "Because I can."

"You're never going to stop, are you? You're so full of rage that you're never going to stop." She shook her head. "Don't hand me that scorpion nonsense. You love to kill. Do you realize how sick that makes you?"

"Sick enough to know I wouldn't be standing here in the rain unless I was sure I'd be able to walk out of here." He glanced around. "This is a nice site for a home. Too bad you'll never build one here. But maybe Paul will bury you here."

"If you think I'm afraid of dying, you're wrong."

"Of course. I am." He spread his lips in a sneer that

was supposed to pass for a smile. "You know where you're going. God and Jesus and all that."

"Death has never frightened me," she admitted. "It's life that strikes terror in my heart. Apparently, in yours, too."

"Spare me your psychobabble. I'd rather be shot."

"That creates a problem."

"Why?"

A calm flooded her deep inside and somehow came through in her voice. "I don't want to kill you."

"Right. And you say I'm crazy?" He snorted. "You want me dead. Don't lie, Maggie. I know you better than you know yourself. You want me dead and buried so you know I'll never bother you or anyone else again."

"At one time I did, but not anymore." Her hands were numbing. She had to get up. She risked rolling into a sitting position. When he didn't shoot, she pulled up to her knees, then to her feet. "I do want you to stop killing." She swiped her hair back from her face. "I want you in jail. Every day for the rest of my life, I want to know that you're there. That your life is as alien to you as you made mine to me."

"Me? In jail?" He aimed at her chest. "That is not happening." He issued her fair warning. "Kill or be killed, Maggie Mason."

He meant it. *Oh, God, please.* She didn't want to kill him. She didn't—

She glimpsed Ian and Detective Cray through the trees. She had to stall Crawford. Keep him talking. "You're not going to kill me. You kill to save people." Ian moved closer. A few more seconds. That's all he or Cray needed. Just a few more seconds. "This isn't saving me, it's saving you."

"Saving you?" He harrumphed. "After all the trouble you've been?"

Ian eased into place behind the thick trunk of an oak. Cray squatted in a clump of palmettos. "Trouble I've been. You stole my life."

Ian and Cray exchanged hand signals and Cray raised up. Maggie's heart seemed to stop, time suspended. Simultaneously, they lunged.

Crawford went down. The gun in his hand fired. Maggie dropped and rolled aside. A stray bullet shattered a branch above her head and it toppled to the ground.

"Let go of me. Now!" Crawford's screams split the sounds of rain, penetrating the blood gushing through her on an adrenaline surge.

Ian jerked Crawford to his feet.

"Kill me. I got your wife. Kill me."

Ian struggled with it. He wanted to kill Crawford, and for a second, Maggie wasn't sure which way he'd go.

"No," Ian said. "No, you live. You live a long, long time and you think about all the lives you've destroyed." He turned to look at Cray. "Cuff him and get him out of my sight before I change my mind."

Cray cuffed Crawford and he and an armed Warny escorted him to Cray's car. As they walked away, Cray called in the capture. The FBI task force would no doubt be waiting for Crawford when he arrived at the station.

Ian eyed Maggie. "Are you all right?"

"I'm fine."

"You sure?" Ian asked. "He didn't hurt you?"

He'd hurt her every day of her life for over three years. "No, not this time."

"Why didn't you shoot him?" Maggie asked Ian. He had to have heard Crawford admit killing Beth.

"I nearly did. But vengeance isn't mine and killing him wasn't necessary. He'll pay for his crimes."

"You heard that he's connected to the Nest."

Ian nodded. "Through Homeland Security." Ian clasped her arms. "You're really okay?"

She nodded, wrapped her arms around Ian and held on tight.

Ian kissed her hard, and then glared at her. "I'm pretty ticked off at you. You led me on a wild-goose chase down to the creek."

She couldn't deny it.

"You knew where he was because you heard the church bells on the phone with him."

She nodded. "That's why I chose this as the site for my home. Every night, you can hear the church bells here."

"You lied to me, Maggie."

"No, I just didn't tell you—"

"That's a lie by omission, and you know it." He frowned. "You've got to stop that."

She clutched his shirtfront, stroked his face. "I couldn't put you in his path, Ian. Not Beth and then you. I love you."

"I love you, too." He kissed her again, pulling her close. When their mouths parted, he warned her, "But if you ever do anything like that again, putting yourself in that kind of danger, we're going to have a big problem."

Bluster. He was scared for her. Still shaking. But he loved her and he'd forgiven her. Maybe there was a slim chance he'd fall in love with her after all.

"Unit's on the way to escort Cray in with him,"

Warny said. "Could take a while because of the roads. They're iced up pretty bad."

"We should stay with Cray. He could try something—Crawford, I mean."

Her uncle stepped out from a thicket of bushes, his shotgun in hand, wearing a camouflage slicker. "He's staying put, sweet pea."

Ian frowned at Warny. "You had your gun?"

"I usually have my gun. Rattlers out here and all."

"Why didn't you shoot him?"

"She was handling it. Three years of running...I figured Maggie needed to take care of him herself." Uncle Warny gave Ian a sidelong look. "If I needed to, I'd a shot him."

Maggie saw straight through that bit of business. Uncle Warny hadn't shot Crawford because of Ian. Ian had been ripped to shreds inside at not being there for Beth when she needed him. He needed to be there for Maggie, and Uncle Warny knew it.

She didn't mention that, but Ian would figure it out. Tomorrow, maybe the next day, the truth would hit him.

"Well." Warny hiked his gun on his shoulder. "I'll feel better if we stick close to Cray until his backup gets here."

The three walked over to the patrol car near the ranch house and joined the detective, then talked about everything that happened. Maggie slid her gaze to the hunched heap kicking up a ruckus in the backseat of the patrol car. Gary Crawford was going to jail for the rest of his life. His reign of terror was finally over.

And Maggie still didn't dare allow herself to shed a single tear.

"Do you know, this is the first midnight in three years that I haven't dreaded hearing my phone ring?"

Maggie looked at Ian seated beside her on the sofa. They'd been Christmas-tree gazing in total silence for nearly an hour, absorbing all that had happened and how quickly their lives had changed.

"I'm glad." Ian's arm lay stretched over her shoulder and he absently rubbed the sleeve of her silky blouse with the tips of his fingers. "It's been a long couple years for us both, but mostly for you."

"We've had our challenges." She leaned her head into his shoulder and chest. His heart beat slow and steady near her ear.

"Yes, we have." He started to say something, stopped and fell silent.

"No more cookies, buddy." Uncle Warny's voice carried through to the living room from the kitchen.

"You know that means he's giving Jake another one, right?" Ian asked Maggie.

"I know." She smiled, looked up at Ian. "I'm so glad you're here."

The look in his eyes warmed. "So am I." He glanced at the tree, then back at her. "Maggie, I need to know you're not blaming yourself for what Crawford did to Beth. You shouldn't be. I know you loved her."

A lump rose in Maggie's throat. "I did. So did you. If I could trade places—"

He pressed his fingers against her lips. "No. It was her time or it wouldn't have happened." He paused a second, then another. "It's time for both of us to move on now. To be at peace with all this."

She was so ready for peace. "Can we do that?" she dared to ask. "Together, I mean?"

"I sure hope so because I can't imagine my life without you."

Don't make more of that than there is. Being in his

*life doesn't mean being in his heart as more than close
friends. Loving, yes. In love, no. No, it didn't mean that
to him.* "Me, either." She swiped her hair back from her
face. "But things are different now. You're not caught
in that awful place of not knowing what happened and
I'm not running, praying I won't get caught and Crawford won't kill again. It's a new start for both of us."

A strange look crossed Ian's face, one she couldn't
decipher. Before she could ask, he changed the subject.

"It doesn't look as if anyone's going to get back for
Christmas."

"Paul and Della are trying." If the icy roads didn't
land them in a ditch, there was a chance they'd get
home.

Ian looked back at her. "Madison, too, with Grant,
but it's not looking promising for them. Passengers on
the ship are lined up, trying to fly off. Rough seas have
made that cruise anything but fun."

She reached for his hand on his thigh. Laced their
fingers. "Would it be so awful if it was just the four of
us—Uncle Warny and Jake, you and me?"

"It wouldn't be your merriest Christmas." He drew
back to look her full in the face. "I'm still ticked off at
you, you know."

"I know." She sat up. "But what was I supposed to
do, Ian? Put you right in the path of a man who would
kill you for the kick of seeing me devastated by it?"

"You'd be devastated?"

"Don't be ridiculous. I love you. Of course I'd be
devastated." She lifted a hand. "I couldn't send you to
him and watch him kill you or try to kill you. I'd rather
he shot me."

"Well, put yourself in my shoes. I love you, too, you
know."

"I know. And I'm sorry you're upset, but I won't lie and say I'd do anything different. I couldn't—not and live with myself." She sniffed. "Just so I'm clear, you did decide not to shoot him. It was your choice. So why are you still ticked?"

"He had a gun aimed at you. He could have shot you, Maggie. Then you'd be gone, too." He grunted. "Good grief, can't you see why I'd be upset about this?"

"That's been established, and no, actually, I can't."

"Well, give me a few days to get my heart back in my chest and I'll explain it to you."

"All right." She agreed, but she wasn't sure if that was a conversation she should eagerly anticipate or dread.

The thing about serial killers is that, once they're caught, they'll confess to anything. Whether or not they're guilty, they'll take blame and claim credit on all they can to elevate their stature, their inflated sense of self-importance, the fear of them in others.

Gary Crawford, aka Daniel L. Ford, had been no exception. He'd taken blame and claimed credit for murdering David Pace, Beth Crane and so much more that was possible for him to have done, including acts against Maggie's brother, Paul, and his fiancée, Della Jackson, but he hadn't.

And that suited the real Mr. Blue Shoes just fine.

Actually, it was better than fine. Because Crawford worked for Homeland Security and had access to the Nest and had actually been there on multiple occasions in his official capacity, which was highly classified, he made the perfect fall guy for the security breach that put the promotions essential to him at risk. The Talbot congressional appointment was looking good. The

Dayton command of the Nest appointment was looking good, and maybe now with the security breach investigation officially closed, the promotions would go through quickly.

That didn't just suit the real Mr. Blue Shoes—it made him deliriously happy. He'd gotten away with murder, and now no one would ever know the truth, because Crawford had claimed responsibility. Inside, Blue Shoes laughed. *Brilliant plan. Absolutely brilliant.*

He walked into Miss Addie's Café and took a seat at the table in the corner near the door and then waited. With the exception of Paul and Della, the staff from Lost, Inc., had returned to North Bay and should arrive momentarily for a "Crawford capture" celebration lunch. Blue Shoes would be celebrating with them... they just wouldn't know it.

Maggie and Ian arrived first. Mrs. Renault, Madison's assistant, came in with the youngest investigator, Jimmy. They were all seated at a long table when Madison and Grant came in. She looked elated and he looked exhausted.

Now what was up with him? Blue Shoes could well imagine. Being stranded on a ship with Madison McKay for five days when she was bent on getting off it...the man had done well, remaining upright.

Miss Addie served him a slice of key lime pie with extra whipped cream, just as he liked it, refilled his coffee cup and then dropped a pat to his shoulder before joining the group.

They didn't have a clue. None of them. They were sharp—some of the best he'd ever commanded—but still, even combined, they hadn't outsmarted him. He took a bite of pie; let the sweet and tangy flavors roll around on his tongue. True, a slight element of luck had broken his way. But tricking all of them…?

Crawford was a clever dog. A killer through and through either bent on enhancing his legacy or using Beth Crane's murder as a final way to create strife between Maggie and Ian. Even a blind man would know they were in love.

It'd been ridiculously easy to position Crawford to take the fall, of course. The one thing that had concerned Blue Shoes was witnesses to his phone call to Brett Lund. Lund's secretary and Jesse, the station's security guard, could have been problematic. She could have recognized his voice. But lucky for her, she hadn't. Still, who could have predicted the station manager would wig out over connecting David Pace and Beth Crane's deaths to the Nest and kill himself?

But Blue Shoes was nothing if not flexible. No one made it to his position without learning how to sidestep a couple of land mines. Now any authority could look all they liked. Officially, on the record, that phone call never came into the station. Oh, Lund's secretary and Jesse knew a call had come in, but the records proving it had been successfully eradicated. The coroner had responded exactly as planned, had told Cray the truth, and Maggie and Ian had pegged Crawford with the murders. So that, too, had worked out exactly as planned.

Which had left Blue Shoes with one challenge. The security breach.

At the moment, the Lost, Inc., team blamed that on Crawford, too. It'd been easy to plant him in the system as an operative for Homeland Security. All it had taken was a few well-placed records that could disappear as quickly as they had appeared—after he'd taken the legal hit for tracking Maggie Mason's every move for three years, breaching his chain of command. Tying Crawford to the Nest put those records in a need-to-know classification that would be seen by few, but would resolve the matter in the minds of many.

Satisfied, Blue Shoes sat back in his seat, sipped at his coffee and then took another bite of the tart pie. Oh, yeah. Crawford was the perfect fall guy. And he was a killer, after all, and as crazy as a loon. The world was better off with him tucked away in prison until he died. Even if at some point in the future he elected to dispute his connection to Homeland Security or to the David Pace or Beth Crane murders, or he later denied putting the neon blue shoes on Pace after his death on the Nest's perimeter, who'd believe him? No one.

But, as Blue Shoes stared across the crowded café to the stunning blonde he loved to hate, there was still a problem. Madison McKay.

At some point, stalling tactics would fail and the beautiful owner of Lost, Inc., would get the satellite images of the base Maggie had requisitioned be sent to Madison. When she did, she'd know far too much about the Nest. She'd see the amount of construction going on and she'd know that no one outside the direct command could do what Crawford purportedly had done—regardless of what the records showed. She'd be a problem.

Which meant she had to go.

Congressional appointments and base commands didn't come along every day, and no one, not even Madison McKay, would be allowed to get in the way of them. He wanted that job. He'd sacrificed for two decades and earned that job, and he was going get it.

He'd handle Madison McKay. She'd be dispatched soon enough.

But today was for celebrating. He polished off the last bite of pie. They were none the wiser and considered everything all tied up in a perfect little bow.

Merry Christmas to me.

"What's the matter, Maggie?"

Leaning against Ian's shoulder, she took her gaze from the lit Christmas tree in the corner of the living room and risked a look at him. "It's been three days. I keep waiting for you to explain, but I'm torn. I'm not sure it'll be an explanation I want to hear so I'm…"

"Worrying."

She nodded.

"Me, too," he confessed, sliding a hand down the thigh of his slacks. "If I knew how you'd react…I guess that's why you're worried, too. You don't know what's coming."

"Exactly."

"It's simple but complex, Maggie."

"Your faith crisis?"

He shook his head no. "I see the error of my ways on that. It's Beth."

Her heart nearly stopped. "You do blame me for Crawford killing her."

"No, I don't. It's just that I loved her with all my heart. You know I did."

She nodded. And he didn't love her. She had been a substitute for Beth, because she'd loved her, too.

"When she died, I thought I'd die, too. I'm ashamed to admit how many times I wished I would, but I did, Maggie. It hurt so deep, in places I can't even name. I never thought one body could hold that much pain."

"But you did hold it."

He nodded. "I felt so guilty for failing her. So guilty

that she was such a good wife and she was dead and I was a lousy husband and I was still alive. It didn't seem fair to take joy in anything, to want or need anything, to care about anything—or about anyone."

"Survivor's guilt—"

"Is only part of it." He paused and focused on the tree, as if emptying his heart like this was too difficult to do while looking at her. "We've been there for each other since Beth died. Grief brought us closer. Well, grief and a need to share whatever was left of us with someone who got what we were going through. But both of us were shells, Maggie. I was because of Beth, and you were because of Crawford." Ian clasped her hand. "Do you know how many nights your emails got me through? It was as if you had this special gift. You knew when I was at rock bottom, and somehow you got me through it. I still don't know how you did that."

"I didn't know I did." What did all this mean? "So what you're saying is that you love me out of gratitude but it's nothing more than that?"

"I do, but no. That's not what I'm saying. I think we started out loving each other out of gratitude, but long before you came back home, things started to change, and when we took that first walk on the ranch—you were barefoot and it was cold out—things really started changing then. And I felt so…"

"Guilty," she speculated. "Because you were alive and feeling again and Beth was dead."

He nodded yes. "But at the cemetery, when you reminded me she didn't need me anymore, that's when my whole world—and my attitude—shifted."

"What exactly do you mean?"

"It occurred to me that Blue Shoes could have killed you and if he had…" Ian's voice faded.

"What?" She waited, but he still didn't answer. "Ian, what?" she asked again.

He looked at her. Pain shimmered in his eyes. "I re-alized it would hurt as much as losing Beth."

"Because…?" Maggie didn't dare make the leap to what she prayed he was saying. She didn't dare.

He dipped his chin so they sat nearly nose to nose. "Because I love you and I'm in love with you, Mag-gie Mason. In that moment, I knew it, and it scared me half to death."

Her mouth went dry. "I can see where that'd be daunting. But intense situations often trick us into thinking we're feeling emotions that—"

"I know that. Which is why I told you to give me three days. I didn't want to hurt you and I don't want to be hurt. I had to be sure what I was feeling wasn't just because of our circumstance, that it was real."

And he'd discovered it wasn't, which is why he hadn't brought it up. Her heart shattered. Why, oh, why, had she pushed him into talking about this? Why?

"You look upset." He sighed. "You don't want me to love and be in love with you?"

That question wasn't expected. "I want to know where you stand now." At least, she thought she did. Did she have the courage to hope? "Was it real, Ian? Do you love me and are you in love with me?"

He cupped her face in his big hands. "I am. Maggie, I am so in love with you that even without a license to dream, I'm dreaming."

Her heart soared. "You are?"

He nodded.

"What are you dreaming?"

"Of you and me together for the rest of our lives. Of us building a beautiful house on your homesite where

we can hear the church bells every night and raise a
family and be deliriously happy."

Maggie couldn't breathe. Didn't dare breathe. Maybe
it was adrenaline. Maybe it was the shock of everything
that happened. "Are you serious?" Her mouth went dry.
"You're dreaming my dreams and you're honestly in
love with me?"

"I am—and don't try to tell me I'm not. I have been
for a long time. I was just confused. When a man never
expects to love again discovers that he already does
and he didn't know it, it is confusing." He sobered, his
voice dropping an octave. "So are you going to keep
me in suspense the rest of my days or tell me—am I
dreaming alone?"

"Oh, Ian." She hugged him hard. "Of course not. I'm
in love with you, too."

"I hoped."

"You did?" She'd been too terrified he wouldn't love
her back to risk hoping.

"I know the exact second I dared to hope."

"When?" She couldn't believe it. Her mind just
wouldn't wrap around it. All she wanted was within reach.

"The moment I realized you'd sent me away from
Crawford and you were facing him alone. You were
protecting me because you'd taken me into your heart,
because that's what you do." He dipped his chin. "Don't
ever do that again, by the way. Whatever we face, we
face it together."

Bemused, she couldn't find her voice but settled for
a nod.

"I was scared to death he'd kill you before I could
tell you."

"Or before you could wring my neck for letting you
go to the creek."

"That, too." He smiled. "But I am really glad you didn't die."

"So am I. Spares your arm—from throwing rocks at my grave every day." Maggie tilted her head and received his kiss.

"Ahem." Uncle Warny cleared his throat. "Sorry to interrupt you two, but you ain't sitting under no mistletoe, so this smooching ain't official, and I got me a surprise for you I figure you'll want to be seeing."

"But we exchange gifts in the morning." Maggie didn't understand. They'd officially held off exchanging gifts until everyone who'd been stranded had time to shop.

He grunted. "You'll be wanting this gift right now."

From behind him, Paul walked in and held his arms open.

Squealing her delight, Maggie sprung up off the sofa and flung herself at her big brother. They hugged long and hard, and Maggie saw Uncle Warny dabbing at his eyes with the edge of his red-and-white bandanna.

Della let out a delicate sniff. "Hi, Ian."

He watched the reunion, his gaze fixed on Maggie. "Welcome home, Della."

Paul put Maggie down on the floor and she hugged Della then grabbed her hand. "Let me see." She shot her brother a warning look. "Paul Mason, there'd better be…" Maggie let out another squeal of pure delight. "Oh, yay! You're engaged. I'm so happy. Ian! Ian, look. She's wearing an engagement ring!"

Congratulations were shared and accepted amid laughter and smiles and heartfelt joy.

Paul hugged his sister again. "It's over, Maggie. Finally, it's over."

"You know?" How was that possible? He'd been without phone service...

"As soon as I heard he was in custody on the radio, I knew what had happened."

"Not exactly, Paul. But I'll fill you in on the details," Uncle Warny said. "Let's get you and Della something hot to drink. Me and Jake was sipping us some hot chocolate. It ain't as good as Della's, but it'll do when it's freezing out."

Paul stilled, stared at his sister. "It's almost too much to take in, isn't it? It being over, I mean."

Crawford had ruled her life and affected Paul's for such a long time. "It's over," she assured him and tugged Ian close, then wrapped an arm around his waist. "And it's just beginning."

Paul looked from her to Ian and back again. "What does that mean?" Paul frowned. "Maggie, you're crying. But you never cry unless..." He shot a warning look at Ian.

"Oh, no." Uncle Warny sighed like the dying. Even Jake made tracks for the kitchen. "I'm outta here. When she gets going, I can't stand it. Maybe if she cried more often it wouldn't be as bad, but rare as it is, it rips this old man's heart to shreds."

"It's okay, Uncle Warny," she assured him. "These are happy tears. I'm...happy." Maggie smiled. "We're all here and together and—"

Paul looked totally lost. "That makes you cry?"

Ian laughed, closed his arms around her and held Maggie while she wept. "Of course it does," he told Paul.

"I'm missing something here." Paul scratched his head.

"Well, when you get it, come tell me and Della and Jake. We'll be in the kitchen."

"Silly cowards." Maggie laughed through her tears. "It just means that I'm getting my merry Christmas."

"Go get some hot chocolate, Paul." Ian winked. "I'll take care of her until she's normal again."

Paul crossed his chest with his arms. "That could take a while."

Ian nodded. "About a lifetime, I figure."

Paul's eyebrows shot up. "Seriously?"

"Oh, yeah."

"Well, all right. Congratulations." Paul looked at his little sister. "Welcome home, Maggie."

She nodded, sobbed, soaking the front of Ian's shirt.

He rubbed circles on her back. "It's okay, honey."

"It's not okay. It's wonderful. I thought I'd never know anything wonderful again, and now everything I ever dreamed of is right here and it's…it's…"

"Wonderful." Over her head, he motioned to Paul to go on.

Smiling, Paul slipped into the kitchen.

Ian pressed his lips to her crown. "You cry, Maggie. It's safe to cry now. You can be weak and vulnerable and it's okay. I've got you now, and I'll be strong for us both for a while and you can finally rest."

"You understand even that—that I couldn't cry or fall apart because if I did…"

He cupped her face in his hand. "Of course, I understand."

Sheer relief washed over her face. "I do love you, Ian."

"I know."

She sniffed. "You're going to have to quit that, you arrogant thing. Say I love you, too."

"It's not arrogant." He cupped her face in his hands. "You have no idea how much it means to me to know you love me." He kissed her forehead, the edge of her brow. "Let me enjoy it just for a while."

That admission changed her whole way of thinking. "Okay." She settled in, her arms around him, his arms around her, and let her emotions settle. The Christmas Countdown was over, and its gifts truly had just begun.

* * * * *

*Don't miss the next thrilling story
in Vicki Hinze's* LOST, INC., *miniseries,
TORN LOYALTIES.
On sale February 2013.*

Dear Reader,

In some way, all of us have experienced doing without to give to someone else. Maybe a friend in trouble, maybe a loved one at risk, or maybe someone hungry on the street. We willingly chose to deny ourselves for their benefit.

That's the heart of Maggie Mason in *Christmas Countdown*. Maggie loves her home, her family and her life, but when a twisted soul threatens it and her, she forfeits all but her life to protect those she loves. Yet for three long years, the twisted soul continues to torment her. It seems things get worse, not better. I say seems, because we too often discover what we see is only a part of the bigger picture and in that bigger picture is something very good. So it is for Maggie.

She does what she has to do and keeps walking in faith. And in her darkest hours, she keeps reaching out to a friend as isolated and alone and wounded as she is—Dr. Ian Crane, a widower craving an elusive peace.

Together they discover that when you dare to care, love can find a way to blossom and grow...and heal.

That's the story of Maggie and Ian. It moved me deeply, and I hope it also moves you.

May you and yours have a joyous Christmas!

Blessings,
Vicki Hinze

Questions for Discussion

1. Maggie must leave all that is familiar to her—her home, family and friends—to protect them. Have you had to forfeit something meaningful to you for the sake of someone else?

2. When in danger, Ian didn't ask for his own protection, he asked for protection for his wife. When he lost her, he was angry with God and he remained so for a long time. Have you been angry with God? How did you work through that?

3. Christmas traditions become all the more dear to Maggie when she's alone and isolated from family and friends. What Christmas traditions do you hold most dear? What makes them so important to you?

4. The villain in Christmas Countdown is a twisted soul, he claims due to the way he was raised. For all intents and purposes, Maggie, too, was raised by absentee parents, yet she became a very different person. What do you think made the difference? Was it the love of Paul, her brother? Her free will choice? Her relationship with God? All of those things, or something else?

5. Ian suffers survivor's guilt and it becomes a major obstacle in his life. He doesn't feel worthy to love, to feel joy, to be happy or content or at peace. And yet he finds his way back to life and heals. Have you ever felt unworthy? Wounded by life and healed?

6. Maggie's brother, Paul, played a parental role in her life. Being younger, Maggie later realized the precious gift he'd given her in always letting her know she was loved. And she wonders then, who had loved Paul? Uncle Warny loves them both, and while he wasn't there from the start, he was there when needed. Have you had an Uncle Warny in your life? Someone who came when needed and supported and gave you strength? Someone who loved you when you most needed to know you were loved?

7. Crawford takes credit for crimes he didn't commit. He wants the blame for these crimes and feels his actions spare his victims. Maggie equates the way Crawford sees things to reflections in a broken mirror: all the pieces are there but they look differently when viewed in distorted shards. Do we all view some things through distorted shards? What kind of things? Just painful ones or joyful ones, too?

8. When home is forbidden, everything about it takes on a deeper, more intense meaning. Little things become dear and those aspects of daily life ignored when things are normal become significant. How can we make the little things significant without the tragedy? Can we appreciate more in normal times, and experience gratitude without the conflict?

9. Miss Addie cooks. She makes a special cake for girls who turn thirteen. Are there special things you do in your family to celebrate significant times in the lives of your family members? Your friends?

10. Crawford made Maggie and Ian miserable. He was, they believe, the one who had cost them both dearly. Yet when both of them had the opportunity to kill him, neither took it. Both opted to forgo vengeance and seek justice. The temptation had to be strong to exact revenge. What do you think gave them the will and strength to opt not to exercise it? What would give you the strength and will to opt for justice?

COMING NEXT MONTH
from Love Inspired® Suspense
AVAILABLE JANUARY 2, 2013

TRACKING JUSTICE
Texas K-9 Unit
Shirlee McCoy
Police detective Austin Black assures Eva Billows he'll find her son. With his search and rescue bloodhound Justice, Austin and Eva search all of Sagebrush, Texas. Eva trusts no one, but Austin—and Justice—won't disappoint her.

THE GENERAL'S SECRETARY
Military Investigations
Debby Giusti
The dying words of the man imprisoned for killing Lillie Beaumont's mother suggest hidden secrets. Special Agent Dawson Timmons agrees. Together, they face painful secrets, but Dawson fears that a murderer is waiting to strike again....

NARROW ESCAPE
Camy Tang
Arissa Tiong and her niece are kidnapped by a notorious drug gang, but Arissa escapes and runs to former narcotics cop Nathan Fischer. He's all that stands between her and the dangerous thugs who are after her.

MIDNIGHT SHADOWS
Carol Post
Escaping a stalker, Melissa Langston flees to her hometown. Only her ex-fiancé, Chris Jamison, a former cop, believes she's still in danger. The more Melissa turns to Chris, the more her stalker wants him gone—permanently.

Look for these and other Love Inspired books wherever books are sold, including most bookstores, supermarkets, discount stores and drugstores.

LISCNM1212

REQUEST YOUR FREE BOOKS!

2 FREE RIVETING INSPIRATIONAL NOVELS
PLUS 2 FREE MYSTERY GIFTS

Love Inspired ®
SUSPENSE

YES! Please send me 2 FREE Love Inspired® Suspense novels and my 2 FREE mystery gifts (gifts are worth about $10). After receiving them, if I don't wish to receive any more books, I can return the shipping statement marked "cancel". If I don't cancel, I will receive 4 brand-new novels every month and be billed just $4.49 per book in the U.S. or $4.99 per book in Canada. That's a saving of at least 22% off the cover price. It's quite a bargain! Shipping and handling is just 50¢ per book in the U.S. and 75¢ per book in Canada.* I understand that accepting the 2 free books and gifts places me under no obligation to buy anything. I can always return a shipment and cancel at any time. Even if I never buy another book, the two free books and gifts are mine to keep forever.

123/323 IDN FEHR

Name	(PLEASE PRINT)	
Address		Apt. #
City	State/Prov.	Zip/Postal Code

Signature (if under 18, a parent or guardian must sign)

Mail to the **Reader Service:**
IN U.S.A.: P.O. Box 1867, Buffalo, NY 14240-1867
IN CANADA: P.O. Box 609, Fort Erie, Ontario L2A 5X3

Not valid for current subscribers to Love Inspired Suspense books.

**Are you a subscriber to Love Inspired Suspense
and want to receive the larger-print edition?
Call 1-800-873-8635 or visit www.ReaderService.com.**

* Terms and prices subject to change without notice. Prices do not include applicable taxes. Sales tax applicable in N.Y. Canadian residents will be charged applicable taxes. Offer not valid in Quebec. This offer is limited to one order per household. All orders subject to credit approval. Credit or debit balances in a customer's account(s) may be offset by any other outstanding balance owed by or to the customer. Please allow 4 to 6 weeks for delivery. Offer available while quantities last.

Your Privacy—The Reader Service is committed to protecting your privacy. Our Privacy Policy is available online at www.ReaderService.com or upon request from the Reader Service.

We make a portion of our mailing list available to reputable third parties that offer products we believe may interest you. If you prefer that we not exchange your name with third parties, or if you wish to clarify or modify your communication preferences, please visit us at www.ReaderService.com/consumerschoice or write to us at Reader Service Preference Service, P.O. Box 9062, Buffalo, NY 14269. Include your complete name and address.

LISUS I I B

Brave police officers tackle crime with the help of their canine partners in TEXAS K-9 UNIT, *an exciting new series from Love Inspired® Suspense.*

Read on for a preview of the first book,
TRACKING JUSTICE by Shirlee McCoy.

Police detective Austin Black glanced at his dashboard clock as he raced up Oak Drive. Two in the morning. Not a good time to get a call about a missing child.

Then again, there was never a good time for that; never a good time to look in the worried eyes of a parent or to follow a scent trail and know that it might lead to a joyful reunion or a sorrowful goodbye.

If it led anywhere.

Sometimes trails went cold, scents were lost and the missing were never found. Austin wanted to bring them all home safe. Hopefully, this time, he would.

He pulled into the driveway of a small house.

Justice whined. A three-year-old bloodhound, he was trained in search and rescue and knew when it was time to work.

Austin jumped out of the vehicle when a woman darted out the front door. "You called about a missing child?"

"Yes. My son. I heard Brady call for me, and when I walked into his room, he was gone." She ran back up the porch stairs.

Austin jogged in after her. She waved from a doorway. "This is my son's room."

Austin followed her into the room. "How old is your son, Ms....?"

"Billows. Eva. He's seven."

"Did you argue?"

"We didn't argue about anything, Officer..."

"Detective Austin Black. I'm with Sagebrush Police Department's Special Operation K-9 Unit."

"You have a search dog with you?" Her face brightened. "I can give you something of his. A shirt or—"

"Hold on. I need to get a little more information first."

"How about you start out there?" She gestured to the window.

"Was it open when you came in the room?"

"Yes. It looks like someone carried Brady out the window. But I don't know how anyone could have gotten into his room when all the doors and windows were locked."

"You're sure?"

"Of course." She frowned. "I always double-check. I have ever since..."

"What?"

"Nothing that matters. I just need to find my son."

Hiding something?

"Everything matters when a child is missing, Eva."

To see Justice the bloodhound in action, pick up
TRACKING JUSTICE by Shirlee McCoy.
Available January 2013 from Love Inspired® Suspense.

Copyright © 2013 by Harlequin Books S.A.

SHLISEXP1212